Robert Browning

Red Cotton Night-Cap Country

Turf and Towers

Robert Browning

Red Cotton Night-Cap Country
Turf and Towers

ISBN/EAN: 9783337230791

Printed in Europe, USA, Canada, Australia, Japan

Cover: Foto ©Andreas Hilbeck / pixelio.de

More available books at **www.hansebooks.com**

RED COTTON NIGHT-CAP COUNTRY

OR

Turf and Towers

BY

ROBERT BROWNING

LONDON
SMITH, ELDER, & CO., 15 WATERLOO PLACE
1873

To

Miss Thackeray

RED COTTON NIGHT-CAP COUNTRY

OR

TURF AND TOWERS

———◦◦◦———

I

AND so, here happily we meet, fair friend !

Again once more, as if the years rolled back

And this our meeting-place were just that Rome

Out in the champaign, say, o'er-rioted

By verdure, ravage, and gay winds that war

Against strong sunshine settled to his sleep ;

B

Or on the Paris Boulevard, might it prove,

You and I came together saunteringly,

Bound for some shop-front in the Place Vendôme—

Gold-smithy and Golconda mine, that makes

" The Firm-Miranda" blazed about the world—

Or, what if it were London, where my toe

Trespassed upon your flouncè? " Small blame," you smile,

Seeing the Stair-case Party in the Square

Was Small and Early, and you broke no rib.

Even as we met where we have met so oft,

Now meet we on this unpretending beach

Below the little village : little, ay !

But pleasant, may my gratitude subjoin ?

Meek, hitherto un-Murrayed bathing-place,

Best loved of sea-coast-nook-ful Normandy !

That, just behind you, is mine own hired house :

With right of path-way through the field in front,

No prejudice to all its growth unsheaved

Of emerald luzern bursting into blue.

Be sure I keep the path that hugs the wall,

Of mornings, as I pad from door to gate !

Yon yellow—what if not wild-mustard flower ?—

Of that, my naked sole makes lawful prize,

Bruising the acrid aromatics out,

Till, what they preface, good salt savours sting

From, first, the sifted sands, then sands in slab,

Smooth save for pipy wreath-work of the worm :

(Granite and muscle-shell are ground alike

To glittering paste,—the live worm troubles yet.)

Then, dry and moist, the varech limit-line,

Burnt cinder-black, with brown uncrumpled swathe

Of berried softness, sea-swoln thrice its size ;

And, lo, the wave protrudes a lip at last,

And flecks my foot with froth, nor tempts in vain.

Such is Saint-Rambert, wilder very much

Than Joyeux, that famed Joyous-Gard of yours,

Some five miles farther down ; much homelier too—

Right for me,—right for you the fine and fair !

Only, I could endure a transfer—wrought

By angels famed still, through our countryside,

For weights they fetched and carried in old time

When nothing like the need was—transfer, just

Of Joyeux church, exchanged for yonder prig,

Our brand-new stone cream-coloured masterpiece.

Well—and you know, and not since this one year,

The quiet seaside country? So do I:

And like it, in a manner, just because

Nothing is prominently likeable

To vulgar eye without a soul behind,

Which, breaking surface, brings before the ball

Of sight, a beauty buried everywhere.

If we have souls, know how to see and use,

One place performs, like any other place,

The proper service every place on earth

Was framed to furnish man with : serves alike

To give him note that, through the place he sees,

A place is signified he never saw,

But, if he lack not soul, may learn to know.

Earth's ugliest walled and ceiled imprisonment

May suffer, through its single rent in roof,

Admittance of a cataract of light

Beyond attainment through earth's palace-panes

Pinholed athwart their windowed filagree

By twinklings sobered from the sun outside.

Doubtless the High Street of our village here

Imposes hardly as Rome's Corso could :

And our projected race for sailing-boats

Next Sunday, when we celebrate our Saint,

Falls very short of that attractiveness,

That artistry in festive spectacle,

Paris ensures you when she welcomes back

(When shall it be ?) the Assembly from Versailles ;

While the best fashion and intelligence

Collected at the counter of our Mayor

(Dry goods he deals in, grocery beside)

What time the post-bag brings the news from Vire,—

I fear me much, it scarce would hold its own,

That circle, that assorted sense and wit,

With Five o'clock Tea in a house we know.

Still, 'tis the check that gives the leap its lift.

The nullity of cultivated souls,

Even advantaged by their news from Vire,

Only conduces to enforce the truth

That, thirty paces off, this natural blue

Broods o'er a bag of secrets, all unbroached,

Beneath the bosom of the placid deep,

Since first the Post Director sealed them safe;

And formidable I perceive this fact—

Little Saint-Rambert touches the great sea.

From London, Paris, Rome, where men are men,

Not mice, and mice not Mayors presumably,

Thought scarce may leap so fast, alight so far.

But this is a pretence, you understand,

Disparagement in play, to parry thrust

Of possible objector : nullity

And ugliness, the taunt be his, not mine

Nor yours,—I think we know the world too well !

Did you walk hither, jog it by the plain,

Or jaunt it by the highway, braving bruise

From springless and uncushioned vehicle ?

Much, was there not, in place and people both,

To lend an eye to ? and what eye like yours—

The learned eye is still the loving one !

Our land ; its quietude, productiveness,

Its length and breadth of grain-crop, meadow-ground,

Its orchards in the pasture, farms a-field

And hamlets on the road-edge, nought you missed

Of one and all the sweet rusticities !

From stalwart strider by the waggon-side,

Brightening the acre with his purple blouse,

To those dark-featured comely women-folk,

Healthy and tall, at work, and work indeed,

On every cottage door-step, plying brisk

Bobbins that bob you ladies out such lace !

Oh, you observed ! and how that nimble play

Of finger formed the sole exception, bobbed

The one disturbance to the peace of things,

Where nobody esteems it worth his while,

If time upon the clock-face goes asleep,

To give the rusted hands a helpful push.

Nobody lifts an energetic thumb

And index to remove some dead and gone

Notice which, posted on the barn, repeats

For truth what two years' passage made a lie.

Still is for sale, next June, that same château

With all its immobilities,—were sold

Duly next June behind the last but last ;

And, woe's me, still placards the Emperor

His confidence in war he means to wage,

God aiding and the rural populace.

No : rain and wind must rub the rags away

And let the lazy land untroubled snore.

Ah, in good truth ? and did the drowsihead

So suit, so soothe the learned loving eye,

That you were minded to confer a crown,

(Does not the poppy boast such ?) call the land

By one slow hither-thither stretching, fast

Subsiding-into-slumber sort of name,

Symbolic of the place and people too,

" *White Cotton Night-cap Country?* " Excellent !

For they do, all, dear women young and old,

Upon the heads of them bear notably

This badge of soul and body in repose ;

Nor its fine thimble fits the acorn-top,

Keeps woolly ward above that oval brown,

Its placid feature, more than muffler makes

A safeguard, circumvents intelligence

In—what shall evermore be named and famed,

If happy nomenclature aught avail,

" *White Cotton Night-cap Country.*"

Do I hear—

Oh, better, very best of all the news—

You mean to catch and cage the winged word,

And make it breed and multiply at home

Till Norman idlesse stock our England too?

Normandy shown minute yet magnified'

In one of those small books, the truly great,

We never know enough, yet know so well?

How I foresee the cursive diamond-dints,—

Composite pen that plays the pencil too,—

As, touch the page and up the glamour goes,

And filmily o'er grain-crop, meadow-ground,

O'er orchard in the pasture, farm a-field

And hamlet on the road-edge, floats and forms

And falls, at lazy last of all, the Cap

That crowns the country! we, awake outside,

Farther than ever from the imminence

Of what cool comfort, what close coverture

Your magic, deftly weaving, shall surround

The unconscious captives with.   Be theirs to drowse

Trammeled, and ours to watch the trammel-trick!

Ours be it, as we con the book of books,

To wonder how is winking possible!

All hail, " White Cotton Night-cap Country," then!

And yet, as on the beach you promise book,—

On beach, mere razor-edge 'twixt earth and sea,

I stand at such a distance from the world

That 'tis the whole world which obtains regard,

Rather than any part, though part presumed

A perfect little province in itself,

When wayfare made acquaintance first therewith.

So standing, therefore, on this edge of things,

What if the backward glance I gave, return

Loaded with other spoils of vagrancy

Than I despatched it for, till I propose

The question—puzzled by the sudden store

Officious fancy plumps beneath my nose—

" Which sort of Night-cap have you glorified ? "

You would be gracious to my ignorance :

" What other Night-cap than the normal one ?—

Old honest guardian of man's head and hair

In its elastic yet continuous, soft,

No less persisting, circumambient gripe,

Night's notice, life is respited from day !

Its form and fashion vary, suiting so

Each seasonable want of youth and age.

In infancy, the rosy naked ball

Of brain, and that faint golden fluff it bears,

Are smothered from disaster,—nurses know

By what foam-fabric; but when youth succeeds,

The sterling value of the article

Discards adornment, cap is cap henceforth

Unfeathered by the futile row on row.

Manhood strains hard a sturdy stocking-stuff

O'er well-deserving head and ears : the cone

Is tassel-tipt, commendably takes pride,

Announcing workday done and wages pouched,

And liberty obtained to sleep, nay, snore.

Unwise, he peradventure shall essay

The sweets of independency for once—

Waive its advantage on his wedding-night :

Fool, only to resume it, night the next,

And never part companionship again.

Since, with advancing years, night's solace soon

Intrudes upon the daybreak dubious life,

Persuades it to appear the thing it is,

Half-sleep; and so, encroaching more and more,

It lingers long past the abstemious meal

Of morning, and, as prompt to serve, precedes

The supper-summons, gruel grown a feast.

Finally, when the last sleep finds the eye

So tired it cannot even shut itself,

Does not a kind domestic hand unite

Friend to friend, lid from lid to part no more,

Consigned alike to that receptacle

So bleak without, so warm and white within?

" Night-caps, night comfort of the human race :

Their usage may be growing obsolete,

Still, in the main, the institution stays.

And though yourself may possibly have lived,

And probably will die, undignified—

The Never-night-capped—more experienced folk

Laugh you back answer—What should Night-cap be

Save Night-cap pure and simple ? Sorts of such ?

Take cotton for the medium, cast an eye

This side to comfort, lambswool or the like,

That side to frilly cambric costliness,

And all between proves Night-cap proper." Add

" Fiddle !" and I confess the argument.

Only, your ignoramus here again

Proceeds as tardily to recognise

Distinctions : ask him what a fiddle means,

And " Just a fiddle " seems the apt reply.

Yet, is not there, while we two pace the beach,

This blessed moment, at your Kensington,

A special Fiddle-Show and rare array

C

Of all the sorts were ever set to cheek,

'Stablished on clavicle, sawn bow-hand-wise,

Or touched lute-fashion and fore-finger-plucked?

I doubt not there be duly catalogued

Achievements all and some of Italy,

Guarnerius, Straduarius,—old and new,

Augustly rude, refined to finicking,

This mammoth with his belly full of blare,

That mouse of music—inch-long silvery wheeze.

And here a specimen has effloresced

Into the scroll-head, there subsides supreme,

And with the tail-piece satisfies mankind.

Why should I speak of woods, grains, stains and streaks,

The topaz varnish or the ruby gum?

We preferably pause where tickets teach

"Over this sample would Corelli croon,

Grieving, by minors, like the cushat-dove,

Most dulcet Giga, dreamiest Saraband."

"From this did Paganini comb the fierce

Electric sparks, or to tenuity

Pull forth the inmost wailing of the wire—

No cat-gut could swoon out so much of soul!"

Three hundred violin-varieties

Exposed to public view! And dare I doubt

Some future enterprise shall give the world

Quite as remarkable a Night-cap-show?

Methinks, we, arm-in-arm, that festal day,

Pace the long range of relics shrined aright,

Framed, glazed, each cushioned curiosity,

And so begin to smile and to inspect :

" Pope's sickly head-sustainment, damped with dews

Wrung from the all-unfair fight—such a frame—

Though doctor and the devil helped their best—

Fought such a world that, waiving doctor's help,

Had the mean devil at its service too !

Voltaire's imperial velvet ! Hogarth eyed

The thumb-nail record of some alley-phiz,

Then chucklingly clapped yonder cosiness

On pate, and painted with true flesh and blood !

Poor hectic Cowper's soothing sarsnet-stripe ! "

And so we profit by the catalogue,

Somehow our smile subsiding more and more,

Till we decline into . . but no ! shut eyes

And hurry past the shame uncoffined here,

The hangman's toilet ! If we needs must trench,

For science' sake which craves completeness still,

On the sad confine, not the district's self,

The object that shall close review may be . . .

Well, it is French, and here are we in France :

It is historic, and we live to learn,

And try to learn by reading story-books.

It is an incident of 'Ninety-two,

And, twelve months since, the Commune had the sway.

Therefore resolve that, after all the Whites

Presented you, a solitary Red

Shall pain us both, a minute and no more !

Do not you see poor Louis pushed to front

Of palace-window, in persuasion's name,

A spectacle above the howling mob

Who tasted, as it were, with tiger-smack,

The outstart, the first spirt of blood on brow,

The Phrygian symbol, the new crown of thorns,

The Cap of Freedom?   See the feeble mirth

At odds with that half-purpose to be strong

And merely patient under misery !

And note the ejaculation, ground so hard

Between his teeth, that only God could hear,

As the lean pale proud insignificance

With the sharp-featured liver-worried stare

Out of the two grey points that did him stead

And passed their eagle-owner to the front

Better than his mob-elbowed undersize,—

The Corsican lieutenant commented

" Had I but one good regiment of my own,

How soon should vollies to the due amount

Lay stiff upon the street-flags this canaille !

As for the droll there, he that plays the king

And screws out smile with a Red night-cap on,

He's done for ! somebody must take his place."

White Cotton Night-cap Country: excellent !

Why not Red Cotton Night-cap Country too ?

" Why not say swans are black and blackbirds white,

Because the instances exist ? " you ask.

" Enough that white, not red, predominates,

Is normal, typical, in cleric phrase

Quod semel, semper, et ubique." Here,

Applying such a name to such a land,

Especially you find inopportune,

Impertinent, my scruple whether white

Or red describes the local colour best.

" Let be," (you say) " the universe at large

Supplied us with exceptions to the rule,

So manifold, they bore no passing-by,—

Little Saint-Rambert has conserved at least

The pure tradition : white from head to heel,

Where is a hint of the ungracious hue ?

See, we have traversed with hop, step and jump,

From heel to head, the main-street in a trice,

Measured the garment (help my metaphor !)

Not merely criticised the cap, forsooth ;

And were you pricked by that collecting-itch,

That pruriency for writing o'er your reds

' Rare, rarer, rarest, not rare but unique,'—

The shelf, Saint-Rambert, of your cabinet,

Unlabelled,—virginal, no Rahab-thread

For blushing token of the spy's success,—

Would taunt with vacancy, I undertake !

What, yonder is your best apology,

Pretence at most approach to naughtiness,

Impingement of the ruddy on the blank?

This is the criminal Saint-Rambertese

Who smuggled in tobacco, half-a-pound !

The Octroi found it out and fined the wretch.

This other is the culprit who dispatched

A hare, he thought a hedgehog, (clods obstruct)

Unfurnished with Permission for the Chase !

As to the womankind—renounce from those

The hope of getting a companion-tinge,

First faint touch promising romantic fault ! "

Enough : there stands Red Cotton Night-cap shelf—

A cavern's ostentatious vacancy—

My contribution to the show; while yours—

White, heaps your row of pegs from every hedge

Outside, and house inside Saint-Rambert here—

We soon have come to end of.   See, the church

With its white steeple gives your challenge point,

Perks as it were the night-cap of the town,

Starchedly warrants all beneath is matched

By all above, one snowy innocence !

You put me on my mettle.   British maid

And British man, suppose we have it out

Here in the fields, decide the question so ?

Then, British fashion, shake hands hard again,

Go home together, friends the more confirmed

That one of us—assuredly myself—

Looks puffy about eye, and pink at nose ?

Which " pink " reminds me that the arduousness

We both acknowledge in the enterprise,

Claims, counts upon a large and liberal

Acceptance of as good as victory

In whatsoever just escapes defeat. `

You must be generous, strain point, and call

Victory, any the least flush of pink

Made prize of, labelled scarlet for the nonce—

Faintest pretension to be wrong and red

And picturesque, that varies by a splotch

The righteous flat of insipidity.

Quick to the quest, then—forward, the firm foot!

Onward, the quarry-overtaking eye!

For what is this, by way of march-tune, makes

The musicalest buzzing at my ear

By reassurance of that promise old

Though sins are scarlet they shall be as wool?

Whence—what fantastic hope do I deduce?

I am no Liebig: when the dyer dyes

A texture, can the red dye prime the white?

And if we washed well, wrung the texture hard,

Would we arrive, here, there and everywhere,

At a fierce ground beneath the surface meek?

I take the first chance, rub to threads what rag

Shall flutter snowily in sight.   For see!

Already these few yards upon the rise,

Our back to brave Saint-Rambert, how we reach

The open, at a dozen steps or strides!

Turn round and look about, a breathing-while!

There lie, out-spread at equidistance, thorpes

And villages and towns along the coast,

Distinguishable, each and all alike,

By white persistent Night-cap, spire on spire.

Take the left : yonder town is—what say you

If I say " Londres "?   Ay, the mother-mouse

(Reversing fable, as truth can and will)

Which gave our mountain of a London birth!

This is the Conqueror's country, bear in mind,

And Londres-district blooms with London-pride.

Turn round : La Roche, to right, where oysters thrive :

Monlieu—the lighthouse is a telegraph;

This, full in front, Saint-Rambert; then succeeds

Villeneuve, and Pons the Young with Pons the Old,

And—ere faith points to Joyeux, out of sight,

A little nearer—oh, La Ravissante !

There now is something like a Night-cap spire,

Donned by no ordinary Notre-Dame !

For, one of the three safety-guards of France,

You front now, lady ! Nothing intercepts

The privilege, by crow-flight, two miles far.

She and her sisters Lourdes and La Salette'

Are at this moment hailed the cynosure

Of poor dear France, such waves have buffeted

Since she eschewed infallibility

And chose to steer by the vague compass-box.

This same midsummer month, a week ago,

Was not the memorable day observed

For reinstatement of the misused Three

In old supremacy for evermore?

Did not the faithful flock in pilgrimage

By railway, diligence and steamer—nay

On foot with staff and scrip, to see the sights

Assured them? And I say best sight was here:

And nothing justified the rival Two

In their pretension to equality;

Our folk laid out their ticket-money best,

And wiseliest, if they walked, wore shoe away;

Not who went farther only to fare worse.

For, what was seen at Lourdes and La Salette

Except a couple of the common cures

Such as all three can boast of, any day? .

While here it was, here and by no means there,

That the Pope's self sent two great real gold crowns

As thick with jewelry as thick could stick,

His present to the Virgin and her Babe—

Provided for—who knows not?—by that fund,

Count Alessandro Sforza's legacy,

Which goes to crown some Virgin every year.

But this year, Pope was in the prison-house,

And money had to go for something else ;

And therefore, though their present seemed the Pope's,

The faithful of our province raised the sum

Preached and prayed out of—nowise purse alone.

Gentle and simple paid in kind, not cash,

The most part : the great lady gave her brooch,

The peasant-girl, her hair-pin ; 'twas the rough

Bluff farmer mainly who,—admonished well

By wife to care lest his new colewort-crop

Stray sorrowfully sparse like last year's seed,—

Lugged from reluctant pouch the fifty-franc,

And had the Curé's hope that rain would cease.

And so, the sum in evidence at length,

Next step was to obtain the donative

By the spontaneous bounty of the Pope—

No easy matter, since his Holiness

Had turned a deaf ear, long and long ago,

To much entreaty on our Bishop's part,

Commendably we boast. " But no," quoth he,

" Image and image needs must take their turn :

Here stand a dozen as importunate."

Well, we were patient; but the cup ran o'er

When—who was it pressed in and took the prize

But our own offset, set far off indeed

To grow by help of our especial name,

She of the Ravissante—in Martinique !

" What ? " cried our patience at the boiling-point,

" The daughter crowned, the mother's head goes bare ?

Bishop of Raimbaux ! "—that's our diocese—

" Thou hast a summons to repair to Rome,

Be efficacious at the Council there :

Now is the time or never ! Right our wrong !

Hie thee away, thou valued Morillon,

And have the promise, thou who hast the vote !"

So said, so done, so followed in due course

(To cut the story short) this festival,

This famous Twenty-second, seven days since.

Oh, but you heard at Joyeux !   Pilgrimage,

Concourse, procession with, to head the host,

Cardinal Mirecourt, quenching lesser lights:

The leafy street-length through, decked end to end

With August-strippage, and adorned with flags,

That would have waved right well but that it rained

Just this picked day, by some perversity.

And so were placed, on Mother and on Babe,

The pair of crowns : the Mother's, you must see !

Miranda, the great Paris goldsmith, made

The marvel,—he's a neighbour : that's his park

Before you, tree-topped wall we walk toward.

His shop it was, turned out the masterpiece,

Probably at his own expenditure ;

Anyhow, his was the munificence

Contributed the central and supreme

Splendor that crowns the crown itself, The Stone.

Not even Paris, ransacked, could supply

That gem : he had to forage in New-York,

This jeweller, and country-gentleman,

And most undoubted devotee beside !

Worthily wived, too : since his wife it was

Bestowed "with friendly hand"—befitting phrase !

The lace which trims the coronation-robe—

Stiff wear—a mint of wealth on the brocade.

Do go and see what I saw yesterday !

And, for that matter, see in fancy still,

Since . .

        There now ! Even for unthankful me,

Who stuck to my devotions at high-tide

That festal morning, never had a mind

To trudge the little league and join the crowd—

Even for me is miracle vouchsafed !

How pointless proves the sneer at miracles !

As if, contrariwise to all we want

And reasonably look to find, they graced

Merely those graced-before, grace helps no whit,

Unless, made whole, they need physician still.

I—sceptical in every inch of me—

Did I deserve that, from the liquid name

" Miranda,"—faceted as lovelily

As his own gift, the gem,—a shaft should shine,

Bear me along, another Abaris,

Nor let me light till, lo, the Red is reached,

And yonder lies in luminosity!

· Look, lady! where I bade you glance, but now!

Next habitation, though two miles away,—

No tenement for man or beast between,—

That, park and domicile, is country-seat

Of this same good Miranda ! I accept

The augury. Or there, or nowhere else,

Will I establish that a Night-cap gleams

Of visionary Red, not White for once !

" Heaven " saith the sage "is with us, here

    inside

Each man :" " Hell also," simpleness subjoins,

By White and Red describing human flesh.

And yet as we continue, quicken pace,

Approach the object which determines me

Victorious or defeated, more forlorn

My chance seems,—that is certainty at least.

Halt midway, reconnoitre ! Either side

The path we traverse (turn and see) stretch fields

Without a hedge : one level, scallop-striped

With bands of beet and turnip and luzern,

Limited only by each colour's end,

Shelves down,—we stand upon an eminence,—

To where the earth-shell scallops out the sea,

A sweep of semicircle ; and at edge—

Just as the milk-white incrustations stud

At intervals some shell-extremity,

So do the little growths attract us here,

Towns with each name I told you : say, they touch

The sea, and the sea them, and all is said,

So sleeps and sets to slumber that broad blue !

The people are as peaceful as the place.

This, that I call " the path " is road, highway ;

But has there passed us by a market-cart,

Man, woman, child, or dog to wag a tail ?

True, I saw weeders stooping in a field ;

But—formidably white the Cap's extent !

Round again !   Come, appearance promises !

The boundary, the park-wall, ancient brick,

Upholds a second wall of tree-heads high

Which overlean its top, a solid green.

That surely ought to shut in mysteries!

A jeweller—no unsuggestive craft!

Trade that admits of much romance, indeed.

For, whom but goldsmiths used old monarchs pledge

Regalia to, or seek a ransom from,

Or pray to furnish dowry, at a pinch,

According to authentic story-books?

Why, such have revolutionized this land

With diamond-necklace-dealing! not to speak

Of families turned upside-down, because

The gay wives went and pawned clandestinely

Jewels, and figured, till found out, with paste,

Or else redeemed them—how, is horrible!

Then there are those enormous criminals

That love their ware and cannot lose their love,

And murder you to get your purchase back.

Others go courting after such a stone,

Make it their mistress, marry for their wife,

And find out, some day, it was false the while,

As ever wife or mistress, man too fond

Has named his Pilgrim, Hermit, Ace of Hearts.

Beside—what style of edifice begins

To grow in sight at last and top the scene?

That grey roof, with the range of lucarnes, four

I count, and that erection in the midst—

Clock-house, or chapel-spire, or what, above?

Conventual, that, beyond manorial, sure!

And reason good; for Clairvaux, such its name,

Was built of old to be a Priory,

Dependence on that Abbey-for-the-Males

Our Conqueror founded in world-famous Caen,

And where his body sought the sepulture,

It was not to retain : you know the tale.

Such Priory was Clairvaux, prosperous

Hundreds of years ; but nothing lasts below,

And when the Red Cap pushed the Crown aside,

The Priory became, like all its peers,

A National Domain : which, bought and sold

And resold, needs must change, with ownership,

Both outside show and inside use ; at length

The messuage, three-and-twenty years ago,

Became the purchase of rewarded worth

Impersonate in Father—I must stoop

To French phrase for precision's sake, I fear—

Father Miranda, goldsmith of renown :

By birth, a Madrilene, by domicile

And sojourning, accepted French at last.

His energy it was which, trade transferred

To Paris, throve as with a golden thumb,

Established in the Place Vendôme.   He bought

Not building only, but belongings far

And wide, at Gonthier there, Monlieu, Villeneuve,

A plentiful estate : which, twelve years since,

Passed, at the good man's natural demise,

To Son and Heir Miranda—Clairvaux here,

The Paris shop, the mansion—not to say

Palatial residence on Quai Rousseau,

With money, moveables, a mine of wealth—

And young Léonce Miranda got it all.

Ah, but—whose might the transformation be ?

Were you prepared for this, now ?   As we talked,

We walked, we entered the half-privacy,

The partly-guarded precinct : passed beside

The little paled-off islet, trees and turf,

Then found us in the main ash-avenue

Under the blessing of its branchage-roof.

Till, on emergence, what affronts our gaze ?

Priory—Conqueror—Abbey-for-the-Males—

Hey, presto, pass, who conjured all away ?

Look through the railwork of the gate : a park

—Yes, but *à l'Anglaise*, as they compliment !

Grass like green velvet, gravel-walks like gold,

Bosses of shrubs, embosomings of flowers,

Wind you—through sprinkled trees of tiny breed

Disporting, within reach of coverture,

By some habitual acquiescent oak

Or elm, that thinks, and lets the youngsters laugh—

Wind, waft at last your soul that walks the air,

Up to the house-front, or its back perhaps—

Whether façade or no, one coquetry

Of coloured brick and carved stone! Stucco? Well,

The daintiness is cheery, that I know,

And all the sportive floral framework fits

The lightsome purpose of the architect.

Those lucarnes which I called conventual, late,

Those are the outlets in the mansard-roof;

And, underneath, what long light elegance

Of windows here suggests how brave inside

Lurk eyeballed gems they play the eyelids to !

Festive arrangements look through such, be sure !

And now the tower a-top, I took for clock's

Or bell's abode, turns out a quaint device,

Pillared and temple-treated Belvedere—

Pavilion safe within its railed-about

Sublimity of area—whence what stretch,

Of sea and land, throughout the seasons' change,

Must greet the solitary ! Or suppose,

—If what the husband likes, the wife likes too—

The happy pair of students cloistered high,

Alone in April when the Spring arrives !

Or no, he mounts there by himself to meet

Winds, welcome wafts of sea-smell, first white bird

That flaps thus far to taste the land again,

And all the promise of the youthful year ;

Then he descends, unbosoms straight his store

Of blessings in the bud, and both embrace,

Husband and wife, since earth is Paradise,

And man at peace with God.   You see it all ?

Let us complete our survey, go right round

The place : for here, it may be, we surprise

The Priory,—these solid walls, big barns,

Grey orchard-grounds, huge four-square stores for stock,

Betoken where the Church was busy once.

Soon must we come upon the Chapel's self.

No doubt next turn will treat us to . . Aha,

Again our expectation proves at fault !

Still the bright graceful modern—not to say

Modish adornment, meets us : *Parc Anglais*,

Tree-sprinkle, shrub-embossment as before.

See, the sun splits on yonder bauble world

Of silvered glass concentring, every side,

All the adjacent wonder, made minute

And touched grotesque by ball-convexity !

Just so, a sense that something is amiss,

Something is out of sorts in the display,

Affects us, past denial, everywhere.

The right erection for the Fields, the Wood,

(Fields—but *Elysées*, wood—but *de Boulogne*)

Is peradventure wrong for wood and fields

When Vire, not Paris, plays the Capital.

So may a good man have deficient taste;

Since Son and Heir Miranda, he it was

Who, six years now elapsed, achieved the work

And truly made a wilderness to smile.

Here did their domesticity reside,

A happy husband and as happy wife,

Till . . how can I in conscience longer keep

My little secret that the man is dead

I, for artistic purpose, talk about

As if he lived still ?   No, these two years now,

Has he been dead.   You ought to sympathise-

Not mock the sturdy effort to redeem

My pledge, and wring you out some tragedy

From even such a perfect common-place !

Suppose I boast the death of such desert

· My tragic bit of Red ? Who contravenes

Assertion that a tragedy exists

In any stoppage of benevolence,

Utility, devotion above all ?

Benevolent ? There never was his like :

For poverty, he had an open hand

. . Or stop—I use the wrong expression here—

An open purse, then, ever at appeal ;

So that the unreflecting rather taxed

Profusion than penuriousness in alms.

One, in his day and generation, deemed

E

Of use to the community ?   I trust

Clairvaux thus renovate and regalised,

Paris expounded thus to Normandy,

Answers that question.   Was the man devout?

After a life—one mere munificence

To Church and all things churchly, men or mice,—

Dying, his last bequeathment gave, land, goods,

Cash, every stick and stiver, to the Church,

And notably to that church yonder, that

Beloved of his soul, La Ravissante—

Wherefrom, the latest of his gifts, the Stone

Gratefully bore me as on arrow-flash

To Clairvaux, as I told you.

                              " Ay, to find

Your Red desiderated article,

Where every scratch and scrape provokes my White

To all the more superb a prominence !

Why, 'tis the story served up fresh again—

How it befell the restive prophet old

Who came and tried to curse but blessed the

    land.

Come, your last chance ! he disinherited

Children: he made his widow mourn too much

By this endowment of the other Bride—

Nor understood that gold and jewelry

Adorn her in a figure, not a fact.

You make the White I want, so very white,

'Tis I say now—some trace of Red should be

Somewhere in this Miranda-sanctitude !"

Not here, at all events, sweet mocking friend !

For he was childless; and what heirs he had

Were an uncertain sort of Cousinry

Scarce claiming kindred so as to withhold

The donor's purpose though fantastical :

Heirs, for that matter, wanting no increase

Of wealth, since rich already as himself ;

Heirs that had taken trouble off his hands,

Bought that productive goldsmith-business, he,

With abnegation wise as rare, renounced

Precisely at a time of life when youth,

Nigh on departure, bids mid-age discard

Life's other loves and likings in a pack,

To keep, in lucre, comfort worth them all.

This Cousinry are they who boast the shop

Of " Firm-Miranda, London and New-York."

Cousins are an unconscionable kind ;

But these—pretension surely on their part

To share inheritance were too absurd !

" Remains then, he dealt wrongly by his wife,

Despoiled her somehow by such testament?"

Farther than ever from the mark, fair friend !

The man's love for his wife exceeded bounds

Rather than failed the limit.   'Twas to live

Hers and hers only, to abolish earth

Outside—since Paris holds the pick of earth—

He turned his back, shut eyes, stopped ears to all

Delicious Paris tempts her children with,

And fled away to this far solitude—

She peopled solitude sufficiently !

She, partner in each heavenward flight sublime,

Was, with each condescension to the ground,

Duly associate also : hand in hand,

. . Or side by side, I say by preference—

On every good work sidlingly they went.

Hers was the instigation—none but she

Willed that, if death should summon first her lord,

Though she, sad relict, must drag residue

Of days encumbered by this load of wealth—

(Submitted to with something of a grace

So long as her surviving vigilance

Might worthily administer, convert

Wealth to God's glory and the good of man,

Give, as in life, so now in death, effect

To cherished purpose)—yet she begged and prayed

That, when no longer she could supervise

The House, it should become a Hospital:

For the support whereof, lands, goods and cash

Alike will go, in happy guardianship,

To yonder church, La Ravissante : who debt

To God and man undoubtedly will pay.

" Not of the world, your heroine ! "

                                  Do you know

I saw her yesterday—set eyes upon

The veritable personage, no dream ?

I in the morning strolled this way, as oft,

And stood at entry of the avenue.

When, out from that first garden-gate, we gazed

Upon and through, a small procession swept—

Madame Miranda with attendants five.

First, of herself : she wore a soft and white

Engaging dress, with velvet stripes and squares

Severely black, yet scarce discouraging :

Fresh Paris-manufacture ! (Vire's would do ?

I doubt it, but confess my ignorance.)

Her figure ? somewhat small and darlinglike,

Her face ? well, singularly colourless,

For first thing : which scarce suits a blonde, you know.

Pretty you would not call her : though perhaps

Attaining to the ends of prettiness

And somewhat more, suppose enough of soul.

Then she is forty full : you cannot judge

What beauty was her portion at eighteen,

The age she married at.   So, colourless

I stick to, and if featureless I add,

Your notion grows completer : for, although

I noticed that her nose was aquiline,

The whole effect amounts with me to—blank !

I never saw what I could less describe.

The eyes, for instance, unforgettable

Which ought to be, are out of mind as sight.

Yet is there not conceivably a face,

A set of wax-like features, blank at first,

Which, as you bendingly grow warm above,

Begins to take impressment from your breath?

Which, as your will itself were plastic here

Nor needed exercise of handicraft,

From formless moulds itself to correspond

With all you think and feel and are—in fine

Grows a new revelation of yourself,

Who know now for the first time what you want?

Here has been something that could wait awhile,

Learn your requirement, nor take shape before,

But, by adopting it, make palpable

Your right to an importance of your own,

Companions somehow were so slow to see !

—Far delicater solace to conceit

Than should some absolute and final face,

Fit representative of soul inside,

Summon you to surrender—in no way

Your breath's impressment, nor, in stranger's guise,

Yourself—or why of force to challenge you ?

Why should your soul's reflexion rule your soul ?

(" You " means not you, nor me, nor anyone

Framed, for a reason I shall keep suppressed,

To rather want a master than a slave :

The slavish still aspires to dominate !)

So, all I say is, that the face, to me

One blurr of blank, might flash significance

To who had seen his soul reflected there

By that symmetric silvery phantom-like

Figure, with other five processional.

The first, a black-dressed matron—may be, maid

Mature, and dragonish of aspect,—marched;

Then four came tripping in a joyous flock,

Two giant goats and two prodigious sheep

Pure as the arctic fox that suits the snow,

Tripped, trotted, turned the march to merriment,

But ambled at their mistress' heel—for why?

A rod of guidance marked the Châtelaine,

And ever and anon would sceptre wave,

And silky subject leave meandering.

Nay, one great naked sheep-face stopped to ask

Who was the stranger, snuffed inquisitive

My hand that made acquaintance with its nose,

Examined why the hand—of man at least—

Patted so lightly, warmly, so like life !

Are they such silly natures after all ?

And thus accompanied, the paled-off space,

Isleted shrubs and verdure, gained the group ;

Till, as I gave a furtive glance, and saw

Her back-hair was a block of solid gold,

The gate shut out my harmless question—Hair

So young and yellow, crowning sanctity,

And claiming solitude . . can hair be false ?

" Shut in the hair and with it your last hope

Yellow might on inspection pass for Red !—

Red, Red, where is the tinge of promised Red

In this old tale of town and country life,

This rise and progress of a family ?

First comes the bustling man of enterprise,

The fortune-founding father, rightly rough,

As who must grub and grab, play pioneer.

Then, with a light and airy step, succeeds

The son, surveys the fabric of his sire,

And enters home, unsmirched from top to toe.

Polish and education qualify

Their fortunate possessor to confine

His occupancy to the first-floor suite

Rather than keep exploring needlessly

Where dwelt his sire content with cellarage :

Industry bustles underneath, no doubt ;

The supervisor should not sit too close.

Next, rooms built, there's the furniture to buy,

And what adornment like a worthy wife ?

In comes she like some foreign cabinet,

Purchased indeed, but purifying quick

What space receives her, from its traffic-taint.

She tells of other habits, palace-life ;

Royalty may have pried into those depths

Of sandal-wooded drawer, and set a-creak

That pygmy portal pranked with lazuli.

More fit by far, the ignoble were replaced

By objects suited to such visitant,

Than that her dignity be desecrate

By neighbourhood of vulgar table, chair,

Which haply helped old age to smoke and doze.

The end is, an exchange of city stir

And too intrusive burgess-fellowship,

For rural isolated elegance,

Careless simplicity, how preferable !

There one may fairly throw behind one's back

The used-up worn-out past, we want away,

And make a fresh beginning of stale life.

' In just the place '—does anyone object?—

' Where aboriginal gentility

Will scout the upstart, twit him with each trick

Of town, trade-mark that stamps each word and deed,

And most of all resent that here the dirt

Is daubed with money-colour to deceive!'

Rashly objected! Is there not the Church

To intercede and bring benefic truce

At outset? She it is shall equalise

The labourers in the vineyard, last as first.

Pay court to her, she stops impertinence.

' Duke, once your sires crusaded it, we know:

Our friend the newcomer observes, no less, ·

Your chapel, rich with their emblazonry,

Wants roofing—might he but supply the means !

Marquise, you gave the honour of your name,

Titular patronage, abundant will

To what should be an Orphan Institute :

Gave everything but funds, in brief; and these,

Our friend, the lady newly resident,

Proposes to contribute, by your leave !'

Brothers and sisters lie they in thy lap,

Thou none-excluding all-collecting Church !

Sure, one has half a foot i' the hierarchy

Of birth, when 'Nay, my dear,' laughs out the Duke,

'I may be cushion-carrier, but the crown—

Who gave its central glory, I or you?'

When Marquise jokes 'My quest, forsooth?   Each doit

I scrape together goes for Peter-pence

To purvey bread and water in his bonds

For Peter's self imprisoned—Lord, how long?

Yours, yours alone the bounty, dear my dame,

You plumped the purse which, poured into the plate,

Made the Archbishop open brows so broad !

And if you really mean to give that length

Of lovely lace to edge the robe !' . . Ah, friends,

Gem better serves so, than by calling crowd

Round shop-front to admire the million's-worth !

Lace gets more homage than from lorgnette-stare,

And comment coarse to match, (should' one display

One's robe a trifle o'er the baignoire-edge,)

' Well may she line her slippers with the like,

If minded so ! their shop it was, produced

That wonderful *parure*, the other day,

Whereof the Baron said, it beggared him.'

And so the paired Mirandas built their house,

F

Enjoyed their fortune, sighed for family,

Found friends would serve their purpose quite as well,

And come, at need, from Paris—anyhow,

With evident alacrity, from Vire—

Endeavour at the chase, at least succeed

In smoking, eating, drinking, laughing, and

Preferring country, oh so much to town !

Thus lived the husband ; though his wife would sigh

In confidence, when Countesses were kind,

' Cut off from Paris and society ! '

White, White, I once more round you in the ears !

Though you have marked it, in a corner, yours

Henceforth,—red-lettered ' Failure ' very plain,

I shall acknowledge, on the snowy hem

Of ordinary Night-cap !   Come, enough !

We have gone round its cotton vastitude,

Or half-round, for the end 's consistent still,

A *cul-de-sac* with stoppage at the sea.

Here we return upon our steps.   One look

May bid good morning—properly good night—

To civic bliss, Miranda and his mate !

Are we to rise and go ? "

        No, sit and stay !

Now comes my moment, with the thrilling throw

Of curtain from each side a shrouded case.

Don't the rings shriek an ominous " Ha ! ha !

So you take Human Nature upon trust ? "

List but with like trust to an incident

Which speedily shall make quite Red enough

Burn out of yonder spotless napery !

Sit on the little mound here, whence you seize

The whole of the gay front sun-satisfied,

One laugh of colour and embellishment !

Because it was there,—past those laurustines,

On that smooth gravel-sweep 'twixt flowers and sward,—

There tragic death befell ; and not one grace

Outspread before you but is registered

In that sinistrous coil, these last two years

Were occupied in winding smooth again.

"True?"   Well, at least it was concluded so,

Sworn to be truth, allowed by Law as such,

(With my concurrence, if it matter here)

A month ago : at Vire they tried the case.

II

Monsieur Léonce Miranda, then, . . but stay !

Permit me a preliminary word,

And, after, all shall go so straight to end !

Have you, the travelled lady, found yourself

Inside a ruin, fane or bath or cirque,

Renowned in story, dear through youthful dream ?

If not,—imagination serves as well.

Try fancy-land, go back a thousand years,

Or forward, half the number, and confront

Some work of art gnawn hollow by Time's tooth,—

Hellenic temple, Roman theatre,

Gothic cathedral, Gallic Tuileries,

But ruined, one and whichsoe'er you like.

Obstructions choke what still remains intact,

Yet proffer change that's picturesque in turn;

Since little life begins where great life ends,

And vegetation soon amalgamates,

Smooths novel shape from out the shapeless old,

Till broken column, battered cornice block

The centre with a bulk half weeds and flowers,

Half relics you devoutly recognise.

Devoutly recognising,—hark, a voice

Not to be disregarded ! " Man worked here

Once on a time ; here needs again to work ;

Ruins obstruct, which man must remedy."

Would you demur " Let Time fulfil his task,

And, till the scythe-sweep find no obstacle,

Let man be patient?"

. The reply were prompt :

" Glisteningly beneath the May-night moon,

Herbage and floral coverture bedeck

Yon splintered mass amidst the solitude :

Wolves occupy the background, or some snake

Glides by at distance: picturesque enough !

Therefore, preserve it?   Nay, pour daylight in,—

The mound proves swarming with humanity.

There never was a thorough solitude,

Now you look nearer : mortal busy life

First of all brought the crumblings down on pate,

Which trip man's foot still, plague his passage much,

And prove—what seems to you so picturesque

To him is . . but experiment yourself

On how conducive to a happy home

Will be the circumstance, your bed for base

Boasts tessellated pavement,—equally

Affected by the scorpion for his nest,—

·While what o'erroofs bed is an architrave,

Marble, and not unlikely to crush man

To mummy, should its venerable prop,

Some fig-tree-stump, play traitor underneath.

Be wise ! Decide ! For conservation's sake,

Clear the arena forthwith ! lest the tread

Of too-much-tried impatience trample out

Solid and unsubstantial to one blank

Mud-mixture, picturesque to nobody,—

And, task done, quarrel with the parts intact

Whence came the filtered fine dust, whence the crash

Bides but its time to follow. Quick conclude

Removal, time effects so tardily,

Of what is plain obstruction ; rubbish cleared,

Let partial-ruin stand while ruin may,

And serve world's use, since use is manifold.

Repair wreck, stancheon wall to heart's content,

But never think of renovation, pure

And simple, which involves creation too :

Transform and welcome ! Yon tall tower may help

(Though built to be a belfry and nought else)

Some Father Secchi, to tick Venus off

In transit : never bring there bell again,

To damage him aloft, brain us below,

When new vibrations bury both in brick !

Monsieur Léonce Miranda, furnishing

The application at his cost, poor soul !

Was instance how,—because the world lay strewn

With ravage of opinions in his path,

And neither he, nor any friendly wit,

Knew and could teach him which was firm, which frail,

In his adventure to walk straight through life

The partial-ruin,—in such enterprise,

He straggled into rubbish, struggled on,

And stumbled out again observably.

" Yon buttress still can back me up," he judged :

And at a touch down came both he and it.

" A certain statue, I was warned against,

Now, by good fortune, lies well under foot,

And cannot tempt to folly any more : "

So, lifting eye, aloft since safety lay,

What did he light on ? the Idalian shape,

The undeposed, erectly Victrix still !

" These steps ascend the labyrinthine stair

Whence, darkling and on all-fours, out I stand

Exalt and safe, and bid low earth adieu—

For so instructs 'Advice to who would climb :'"

And all at once the climbing landed him

—Where, is my story.

                      Take its moral first.

Do you advise a climber ?   Have respect

To the poor head, with more or less of brains

To spill, should breakage follow your advice !

Head-break to him will be heart-break to you

For having preached " Disturb no ruins here !

Are not they crumbling of their own accord?

Meantime, let poets, painters keep a prize !

Beside, a sage pedestrian picks his way."

A sage pedestrian—such as you and I!

What if there trip, in merry carelessness,

And come to grief, a weak and foolish child?

Be cautious how you counsel climbing, then !

Are you adventurous and climb yourself?

Plant the foot warily, accept a staff,

Stamp only where you probe the standing-point,

Move forward, well assured that move you may :

Where you mistrust advance, stop short and stick !

This makes advancing slow and difficult?

Hear what came of endeavour of brisk youth

To foot it fast and easy !   Keep this same

Notion of outside mound and inside mash,

Towers yet intact round turfy rottenness,

Symbolic partial-ravage,—keep in mind !

Here fortune placed his feet who first of all

Found no incumbrance, till head found . . But hear !

This son and heir then of the jeweller,

Monsieur Léonce Miranda, at his birth,

Mixed the Castilian passionate blind blood

With answerable gush, his mother's gift,

Of spirit, French and critical and cold.

Such mixture makes a battle in the brain,

Ending as faith or doubt gets uppermost ;

Then will has way a moment, but no more,

So nicely-balanced are the adverse strengths,

And victory entails reverse next time.

The tactics of the two are different

And equalize the odds: for blood comes first,

Surrounding life with undisputed faith.

But presently, a new antagonist,

By scarce-suspected passage in the dark,

Steals spirit, fingers at each crevice found

Athwart faith's stronghold, fronts the astonished man :

"Such pains to keep me far, yet here stand I,

Your doubt inside the faith-defence of you!"

With faith it was friends bulwarked him about

From infancy to boyhood ; so, by youth,

Faith stood the impenetrable circuit, high

As heaven and low as hell : what lacked he there,

Guarded against aggression, storm or sap ?

What foe would dare approach ?   Historic Doubt ?

Ay, were there some half-knowledge to attack !

Batter doubt's best, sheer ignorance will beat.

Acumen metaphysic?—drills its way

Through what, I wonder! A thick feather-bed

Of thoughtlessness, no operating tool—

Framed to transpierce the flint-stone—fumbles at,

With chance of finding an impediment!

This Ravissante, now: when he saw the church

For the first time, and to his dying-day,

His firm belief was that the name fell fit

From the Delivering Virgin, niched and known;

As if there wanted records to attest

The appellation was a pleasantry,

A pious rendering of Rare Vissante,

The proper name which erst our province bore.

He would have told you that Saint Aldabert

Founded the church, (Heaven early favoured France,)

About the second century from Christ;

Though the true man was Bishop of Raimbaux,

Eleventh in succession, Eldobert,

Who flourished after some six hundred years.

He it was brought the image " from afar,"

(Made out of stone the place produces still)

" Infantine Art divinely artless," (Art

In the decrepitude of Decadence)

And set it up a-working miracles

Until the Northmen's fury laid it low,

Not long, however : an egregious sheep,

Zealous with scratching hoof and routing horn,

Unearthed the image in good Mailleville's time,

Count of the country. " If the tale be false,

Why stands it carved above the portal plain ? "

Monsieur Léonce Miranda used to ask.

To Londres went the prize in solemn pomp,

But, liking old abode and loathing new,

Was borne—this time, by angels—back again.

And, reinaugurated, miracle

Succeeded miracle, a lengthy list,

Until indeed the culmination came—

Archbishop Chaumont prayed a prayer and vowed

A vow—gained prayer and paid vow properly—

For the conversion of Prince Vertgalant.

These facts, sucked in along with mother's-milk,

Monsieur Léonce Miranda would dispute

As soon as that his hands were flesh and bone,

Milk-nourished two-and-twenty years before.

So fortified by blind Castilian blood,

What say you to the chances of French cold

Critical spirit, should Voltaire besiege

G

"Alp, Apennine, and fortified redoubt?"

Ay, would such spirit please to play faith's game

Faith's way, attack where faith defends so well!

But then it shifts, tries other strategy.

Coldness grows warmth, the critical becomes

Unquestioning acceptance.   "Share and share

Alike in facts, to truth add other truth!

Why with old truth needs new truth disagree?"

Thus doubt was found invading faith, this time,

By help of not the spirit but the flesh:

Fat Rabelais chuckled, where faith lay in wait

For lean Voltaire's grimace—French, either foe.

Accordingly, while round about our friend

Ran faith without a break which learned eye

Could find at two-and-twenty years of age,

The twenty-two-years-old frank footstep soon

Assured itself there spread a standing-space

Flowery and comfortable, nowise rock

Nor pebble-pavement roughed for champion's tread

Who scorns discomfort, pacing at his post.

Tall, long-limbed, shoulder right and shoulder left,

And 'twixt *acromia* such a latitude,

Black heaps of hair on head, and blacker bush

O'er-rioting chin, cheek and throat and chest,—

His brown meridional temperament

Told him—or rather pricked into his sense

Plainer than language—" Pleasant station here!

Youth, strength, and lustihood can sleep on turf

Yet pace the stony platform afterward :

First signal of a foe and up they start !

Saint Eldobert, at all such vanity,

Nay—sinfulness, had shaken head austere.

Had he !   But did Prince Vertgalant ?   And yet,

After how long a slumber, of what sort,

Was it, he stretched octogenary joints

And, nigh on Day-of-Judgment trumpet-blast,

Jumped up and manned wall, brisk as any bee ? "

Nor Rabelais nor Voltaire, but Sganarelle,

You comprehend, was pushing through the chink !

That stager in the saint's correct costume,

Who ever has his speech in readiness

For thick-head juvenility at fault :

" Go pace yon platform and play sentinel !

You won't ?   The worse ! but still a worse might hap.

Stay then, provided that you keep in sight

The battlement, one bold leap lands you by !

Resolve not desperately ' Wall or turf,

Choose this, choose that, but no alternative !'

No ! Earth left once were left for good and all :

'With Heaven you may accommodate yourself.' "

Saint Eldobert—I much approve his mode ;

With sinner Vertgalant I sympathize;

But histrionic Sganarelle, who prompts

While pulling back, refuses yet concedes,—

Whether he preach in chair, or print in book,

Or whisper due sustainment to weak flesh,

Counting his sham beads threaded on a lie—

Surely, one should bid pack that mountebank !

Surely, he must have momentary fits

Of self-sufficient stage-forgetfulness,

Escapings of the actor-lassitude

When he allows the grace to show the grin,

Which ought to let even thickheads recognize

(Through all the busy and benefic part,—

Bridge-building, or rock-riving, or good clean

Transport of church and congregation both

From this to that place with no harm at all,)

The Devil, that old stager, at his trick

Of general utility, who leads

Down-ward, perhaps, but fiddles all the way!

Therefore, no sooner does our candidate

For saintship spotlessly emerge soul-cleansed

From First Communion to mount guard at post,

Paris-proof, top to toe, than up there starts

The Spirit of the Boulevard—you know Who—

With jocund "So, a structure fixed as fate,

Faith's tower joins on to tower, no ring more round,

Full fifty years at distance, too, from youth!

Once reach that precinct and there fight your

best,

As looking back you wonder what has come

Of daisy-dappled turf you danced across !

Few flowers that played with youth shall pester age,

However age esteem the courtesy ;

And Eldobert was something past his prime,

Stocked Caen with churches ere he tried hand here.

Saint-Sauveur, Notre-Dame, Saint-Pierre, Saint-Jean

Attest, his handiwork commenced betimes.

He probably would preach that turf is mud.

Suppose it mud, through mud one picks a way,

And when, clay-clogged, the struggler steps to stone,

He uncakes shoe, arrives in manlier guise

Than carried pick-a-back by Eldobert

Big-baby-fashion, lest his leathers leak !

All that parade about Prince Vertgalant

Amounts to—your Castilian helps enough—

Inveni ovem quæ perierat.

But ask the pretty votive statue-thing

What the lost sheep's meantime amusements were

Till the Archbishop found him !   That stays blank :

They washed the fleece well and forgot the rest.

Make haste, since time flies, to determine, though !"

Thus opportunely took up parable,—

Admonishing Miranda just emerged

Pure from The Ravissante and Paris-proof,—

Saint Sganarelle : then slipped aside, changed mask,

And made re-entry as a gentleman

Born of the Boulevard, with another speech,

I spare you.

So, the year or two revolved,

And ever the young man was dutiful

To altar and to hearth : had confidence

In the whole Ravissantish history.

Voltaire? Who ought to know so much of him,—

Old sciolist, whom only boys think sage,—

As one whose father's house upon the Quai

Neighboured the very house where that Voltaire

Died mad and raving, not without a burst

Of squibs and crackers, too significant?

Father and mother hailed their best of sons,.

Type of obedience, domesticity,

Never such an example inside doors !

Outside, as well not keep too close a watch ;

Youth must be left to some discretion there.

And what discretion proved, I find deposed

At Vire, confirmed by his own words: to wit,

How, with the spriteliness of twenty-five,

Five—and not twenty, for he gave their names

With laudable precision—were the few

Appointed by him unto mistress-ship;

While, meritoriously the whole long week

A votary of commerce only, week

Ended, "at shut of shop on Saturday,

Do, I, as is my wont, get drunk," he writes

In airy record to a confidant.

" Bragging and lies !" replied the apologist :

"And do I lose by that ?" laughed Somebody,

At the Court-edge a-tiptoe, mid the crowd,

In his own clothes, a-listening to men's Law.

Thus while, prospectively a combatant,

The volunteer bent brows, clenched jaws, and fierce

Whistled the march-tune "Warrior to the wall!"

Something like flowery laughters round his feet

Tangled him of a sudden with "Sleep first!"

And fairly flat upon the turf sprawled he

And let strange creatures make his mouth their home.

Anyhow, 'tis the nature of the soul

To seek a show of durability,

Nor, changing, plainly be the slave of change.

Outside the turf, the towers : but, round the turf,

A tent may rise, a temporary shroud,

Mock-faith to suit a mimic dwelling-place :

Tent which, while screening jollity inside

From the external circuit—evermore

A menace to who lags when he should march—

Yet stands a-tremble, ready to collapse

At touch of foot: turf is acknowledged grass,

And grass, though pillowy, held contemptible

Compared with solid rock, the rampired ridge.

To truth, a pretty homage thus we pay

By testifying—what we dally with,

Falsehood, (which, never fear we take for truth!)

We may enjoy, but then—how we despise !

Accordingly, on weighty business bound,

Monsieur Léonce Miranda stooped to play,

But, with experience, soon reduced the game

To principles, and thenceforth played by rule :

Rule, dignifying sport as sport, proclaimed

No less that sport was sport and nothing more.

He understood the worth of womankind,—

To furnish man—provisionally—sport :

Sport transitive—such earth's amusements are :

But, seeing that amusements pall by use,

Variety therein is requisite.

And since the serious work of life were wronged

Should we bestow importance on our play,

It follows, in such womankind-pursuit,

Cheating is lawful chase.   We have to spend

An hour—they want a lifetime thrown away :

We seek to tickle sense—they ask for soul,

As if soul had no higher ends to serve !

A stag-hunt gives the royal creature law :

Bat-fowling is all fair with birds at roost,

The lantern and the clapnet suit the hedge.

Which must explain why, bent on Boulevard game,

Monsieur Léonce Miranda decently

Was prudent in his pleasure — passed himself

Off on the fragile fair about his path

As the gay devil rich in mere good looks,

Youth, hope—what matter though the purse be void ?

" If I were only young Miranda, now,

Instead of a poor clerkly drudge at desk

All day, poor artist vainly bruising brush

On palette, poor musician scraping gut

With horsehair teazed that no harmonics come !

Then would I love with liberality,

Then would I pay !—who now shall be repaid,

Repaid alike for present pain and past,

If Mademoiselle permit the contre-danse,

Sing ' Gay in garret youth at twenty lives,'

And afterward accept a lemonade !"

Such sweet facilities of intercourse

Afford the Winter-Garden and Mabille !

" Oh, I unite "—runs on the confidence,

Poor fellow, that was read in open Court,

—" Amusement with discretion : never fear

My escapades cost more than market-price !

No durably-attached Miranda-dupe,

Sucked dry of substance by two clinging lips,

Promising marriage, and performing it !

Trust me, I know the world, and know myself,

And know where duty takes me—in good time ! "

Thus fortified and realistic, then,

At all points thus against illusion armed,

He wisely did New Year inaugurate

By playing truant to the favoured five :

And sat installed at " The Varieties,"—

Playhouse appropriately named,— to note

(Prying amid the turf that 's flowery there)

What primrose, firstling of the year, might push

The snows aside to deck his button-hole—

Unnoticed by that outline sad, severe,

(Though fifty good long years removed from youth)

That tower and tower,—our image, bear in mind !

No sooner was he seated than, behold,

Out burst a polyanthus ! He was 'ware

Of a young woman niched in neighbourhood ;

And ere one moment flitted, fast was he

Found bondslave to the beauty evermore,

For life, for death, for heaven, for hell, her own.

Philosophy, bewail thy fate !   Adieu,

Youth realistic and illusion-proof !

Monsieur Léonce Miranda,—hero late

Who "understood the worth of womankind,"

" Who found therein—provisionally—sport,"—

Felt, in the flitting of a moment, fool

Was he, and folly all that seemed so wise,

And the best proof of wisdom's birth would be

That he made all endeavour, body, soul,

By any means, at any sacrifice

Of labour, wealth, repute, and (—well, the time

For choosing between heaven on earth, and heaven

In heaven, was not at hand immediately—)

Made all endeavour, without loss incurred

Of one least minute, to obtain her love.

" Sport transitive ?" " Variety required ?"

" In loving were a lifetime thrown away?"

How singularly may young men mistake !

The fault must be repaired with energy.

Monsieur Léonce Miranda ate her up

With eye-devouring ; when the unconscious fair

Passed from the close-packed hall, he pressed behind ;

She mounted vehicle, he did the same,

Coach stopped, and cab fast followed, at one door—

Good house in unexceptionable street.

Out stepped the lady,—never think, alone !

A mother was not wanting to the maid,

Or, may be, wife, or widow, might one say ?

Out stepped and properly down flung himself

Monsieur Léonce Miranda at her feet—

And never left them after, so to speak,

For twenty years, till his last hour of life,

When he released them, as precipitate.

Love proffered and accepted then and there !

Such potency in word and look has truth.

Truth I say, truth I mean : this love was true,

And the rest happened by due consequence.

By which we are to learn that there exists

A falsish false, for truth's inside the same,

And truth that's only half true, falsish truth.

The better for both parties ! folks may taunt

That half your rock-built wall is rubble-heap :

Answer them, half their flowery turf is stones !

Our friend had hitherto been decking coat

If not with stones, with weeds that stones befit,

With dandelions—" primrose-buds," smirked he ;

This proved a polyanthus on his breast,

Prize-lawful or prize-lawless, flower the same.

So with his other instance of mistake :

Was Christianity the Ravissante?

And what a flower of flowers he chanced on

    now !

To primrose, polyanthus I prefer

As illustration, from the fancy-fact

That out of simple came the composite

By culture: that the florist bedded thick

His primrose-root in ruddle, bullock's blood,

Ochre and devils'-dung, for aught I know,

Until the pale and pure grew fiery-fine,

Ruby and topaz, rightly named anew.

This lady was no product of the plain ;

Social manure had raised a rarity.

Clara de Millefleurs (note the happy name)

Blazed in the full-blown glory of her Spring.

Peerlessly perfect, form and face : for both—

" Imagine, what, at seventeen, may have proved

Miss Pages, the actress : Pages herself, my dear ! "

Noble she was, the name denotes : and rich?

" The apartment in this Coliseum Street,

Furnished, my dear, with such an elegance,

Testifies wealth, my dear, sufficiently !

What quality, what style and title, eh?

Well now, waive nonsense, you and I are boys

No longer : somewhere must a screw be slack !

Don't fancy, Duchesses descend at door

From carriage-step to stranger prostrate stretched,

And bid him take heart, and deliver mind,

March in and make himself at ease forthwith,—

However broad his chest and black his beard,

And comely his belongings,—all through love

Protested in a world of ways save one

Hinting at marriage!"—marriage which yet means

Only the obvious method, easiest help

To satisfaction of love's first demand,

That love endure eternally: "my dear,

Somewhere or other must a screw be slack !"

Truth is the proper policy: from truth—

Whate'er the force wherewith you fling your

    speech,—

Be sure that speech will lift you, by rebound,

Somewhere above the lowness of a lie !

Monsieur Léonce Miranda heard too true

A tale—perhaps I may subjoin, too trite !

As the meek martyr takes her statued stand

Above our pity, claims our worship just

Because of what she puts in evidence,

Signal of suffering, badge of torture borne

In days gone by, shame then but glory now,

Barb in the breast, turned aureole for the front !

So, half timidity, composure half,

Clara de Millefleurs told her martyrdom.

Of poor though noble parentage, deprived

Too early of a father's guardianship,

What wonder if the prodigality

Of nature in the girl, whose mental gifts

Matched her external dowry, form and face—

If these suggested a too prompt resource

To the resourceless mother ? " Try the Stage

And so escape starvation ! Prejudice

Defames Mimetic Art : be yours to prove

That gold and dross may meet and never mix,

Purity plunge in pitch yet soil no plume !"

All was prepared in London—(you conceive

The natural shrinking from publicity

In Paris, where the name excites remark)

London was ready for the grand debût ;

When some perverse ill fortune, incident

To art mimetic, some malicious thrust

Of Jealousy who sidles 'twixt the scenes

Or pops up sudden from the prompter's hole,—

Somehow the brilliant bubble burst in suds.

Want followed : in a foreign land, the pair !

O hurry over the catastrophe—

Mother too sorely tempted, daughter tried

Scarcely so much as circumvented, say!

Caged unsuspecting artless innocence!

Monsieur Léonce Miranda tell the rest !—

The rather that he told it in a style

To puzzle Court Guide students, much more me.

" Brief, she became the favourite of Lord N.,

An aged but illustrious Duke, thereby

Breaking the heart of his competitor

The Prince of O.   Behold her palaced straight

In splendor, clothed in diamonds," (phrase how fit !)

"Giving tone to the City by the Thames !

Lord N., the aged but illustrious Duke,

Was even on the point of wedding her—

Giving his name to her " (why not to us?)

" But that her better angel interposed.

She fled from such a fate to Paris back,

A fortnight since : conceive Lord N.'s despair !

Duke as he is, there's no invading France.

He must restrict pursuit to postal plague

Of writing letters daily, duly read

As darlingly she hands them to myself,

The privileged supplanter, who therewith

Light a cigar and see abundant blue "—

(Either of heaven or else Havanna-smoke.)

" Think ! she, who helped herself to diamonds late,

In passion of disinterestedness

Now—will accept no tribute of my love

Beyond a paltry ring, three Louis'-worth !

Little she knows I have the rummaging

Of old Papa's shop in the Place Vendôme ! "

So wrote entrancedly to confidant,

Monsieur Léonce Miranda.   Surely now,

If Heaven, that sees all, understands no less,

It finds temptation pardonable here,

It mitigates the promised punishment,

It recognizes that to tarry just

An April hour amid such dainty turf

Means no rebellion against task imposed

Of journey to the distant wall one day !

Monsieur Léonce Miranda puts the case!

Love, he is purposed to renounce, abjure ;

But meanwhile, is the case a common one ?

Is it the vulgar sin, none hates as he ?

Which question, put directly to "his dear"

(His brother—I will tell you in a trice)

Was doubtless meant, by due meandering,

To reach, to fall not unobserved before

The auditory cavern 'neath the cope

Of Her, the placable, the Ravissante.

But here's the drawback, that the image smiles,

Smiles on, smiles ever, says to supplicant

" Ay, ay, ay "—like some kindly weathercock

Which, stuck fast at Set Fair, Favonian Breeze,

Still warrants you from rain, though Auster's lead

Bring down the sky above your cloakless mirth.

Had he proposed this question to, nor " dear "

Nor Ravissante, but prompt to the Police,

The Commissary of his Quarter, now—

There had been shaggy eyebrows elevate

With twinkling apprehension in each orb

Beneath, and when the sudden shut of mouth

Relaxed,—lip pressing lip, lest out should plump

The pride of knowledge in too frank a flow,—

Then, fact on fact forthcoming, dose were dealt

Of truth remedial, in sufficiency

To save a chicken threatened with the pip,

Head-staggers and a tumble from its perch.

Alack, it was the lady's self that made

The revelation, after certain days

—Nor so unwisely! As the haschisch-man

Prepares a novice to receive his drug,

Adroitly hides the soil with sudden spread

Of carpet ere he seats his customer:

Then shows him how to smoke himself about

With Paradise; and only when, at puff

Of pipe, the Houri dances round the brain

Of dreamer, does he judge no need is now

For circumspection and punctiliousness;

He may resume the serviceable scrap

That made the votary unaware of muck.

Just thus the lady, when her brewage—love—

Was well a-fume about the novice-brain,

Saw she might boldly pluck, from underneath

Her lover, the preliminary lie.

Clara de Millefleurs, of the noble race,

Was Lucie Steiner, child to Dominique

And Magdalen Commercy ; born at Sierck,

About the bottom of the Social Couch.

The father having come and gone again,

The mother and the daughter found their way

To Paris, and professed mode-merchandize,

Were milliners, we English roughlier say;

And soon a fellow-lodger in the house,

Monsieur Ulysse Muhlhausen young and smart,

Tailor by trade, perceived his house-mate's youth,

Smartness, and beauty over and above.

Courtship was brief, and marriage followed quick,

And quicklier—impecuniosity.

The young pair quitted Paris to reside

At London : which repaid the compliment

But scurvily, since not a whit the more

Trade prospered by the Thames than by the Seine.

Failing all other, as a last resource,

" He would have trafficked in his wife,"—she said.

If for that cause they quarrelled, ' twas, I fear,

Rather from reclamation of her rights

To wifely independence, than as wronged

Otherwise by the course of life proposed :

Since, on escape to Paris back again,

From horror and the husband,—ill-exchanged

For safe maternal home recovered thus,—

I find her domiciled and dominant

In that apartment, Coliseum Street,

Where all the splendid magic met and mazed

Monsieur Léonce Miranda's venturous eye.

Only, the same was furnished at the cost

Of someone notable in days long since,

Carlino Centofanti : he it was,

Found entertaining unawares—if not

An angel, yet a youth in search of one.

Why this revealment after reticence ?

Wherefore, beginning " Millefleurs," end at all

Steiner, Muhlhausen, and the ugly rest?

Because the unsocial purse-comptrolling wight,

Carlino Centofanti, made aware

By misadventure that his bounty—crumbs

From table—comforted a visitant,

Took churlish leave, and left, too, debts to pay.

Loaded with debts, the lady needs must bring

Her soul to bear assistance from a friend

Beside that paltry ring, three Louis'-worth;

And therefore might the little circumstance

That Monsieur Léonce had the rummaging

Of old Papa's shop in the Place Vendôme,

Pass, perhaps, not so unobservably.

Frail shadow of a woman in the flesh,

These very eyes of mine saw yesterday,

I

Would I re-tell this story of your woes,

Would I have heart to do you detriment

. By pinning all this shame and sorrow plain

To that poor chignon,—staying with me still,

Though form and face have well nigh faded now,—

But that men read it, rough in brutal print,

As two years since some functionary's voice

Rattled all this—and more by very much—

Into the ear of vulgar Court and crowd,

Whence, by reverberation, rumblings grew

To what had proved a week-long roar in France,

Had not the dreadful cannonry drowned all.

Was, now, the answer of your advocate

More than just this? " The shame fell long ago,

The sorrow keeps increasing : God forbid

We judge man, by the faults of youth, in age ! "

Permit me the expression of a hope

Your youth proceeded like your avenue,

Stepping by bush, and tree, and taller tree,

Until, columnar, at the house they end.

So might your creeping youth, columnar rise

And reach, by year and year, symmetrical,

To where all shade stops short, shade's service done.

Bushes on either side, and boughs above,

Darken, deform the path, else sun would streak ;

And, cornered halfway somewhere, I suspect

Stagnation and a horse-pond : hurry past!

For here 's the house, the happy half-and-half

Existence—such as stands for happiness

True and entire, howe'er the squeamish talk !

Twenty years long, you may have loved this man ;

He must have loved you ; that's a happy life,

Whatever was your right to lead the same.

The white domestic pigeon pairs secure,

Nay, does mere duty by bestowing egg

In authorized compartment, warm and safe,

Boarding about, and gilded spire above,

Hoisted on pole, to dogs' and cats' despair !

But I have spied a veriest trap of twigs

On tree-top, every straw a thievery,

Where the wild dove—despite the fowler's snare,

The sportsman's shot, the urchin's stone,—crooned gay,

And solely gave her heart to what she hatched,

Nor minded a malignant world below.

I throw first stone forsooth ?   'Tis mere assault

Of playful sugarplum against your cheek,

Which, if it makes cheek tingle, wipes off rouge !

You, my worst woman ?   Ah, that touches pride,

Puts on his mettle the exhibitor

Of Night-caps, if you taunt him " This, no doubt,—

Now we have got to Female-garniture,—

Crowns your collection, Reddest of the row ! "

O unimaginative ignorance

Of what dye's depth keeps best apart from worst

In womankind !—how heaven's own pure may seem

To blush aurorally beside such blanched

Divineness as the women-wreaths named White:

While hell, eruptive and fuliginous,

Sickens to very pallor as I point

Her place to a Red clout called woman too !

Hail, heads that ever had such glory once

Touch you a moment, like God's cloven tongues

Of fire, your lambent aureoles lost, that leave

You marked yet, dear beyond all diadems !

And hold, each foot, nor spurn, to man's disgrace,

What other twist of fetid rag may fall!

Let slink into the sewer the cupping-cloth!

Lucie, much solaced, I re-finger you,

The medium article; if ruddy-marked

With iron-mould, your cambric,—clean at least

From poison-speck of rot and purulence!

Lucie Muhlhausen said—" Such thing am I:

Love me, or love me not!"   Miranda said

" I do love, more than ever, most for this."

The revelation of the very truth,

· Proved the concluding necessary shake

That bids the tardy mixture crystalize

Or else stay ever liquid : shoot up shaft,

Durably diamond, or evaporate—

Sluggish solution through a minute's slip.

Monsieur Léonce Miranda took his soul

In both his hands, as if it were a vase,

To see what came of the convulsion there,

And found, amid subsidence, love new-born

So sparklingly resplendent, old was new.

" Whatever be my lady's present, past,

Or future, this is certain of my soul,

I love her ! in despite of all I know,

Defiance of the much I have to fear,

I venture happiness on what I hope,

And love her from this day for evermore !

No prejudice to old profound respect

For certain Powers ! I trust they bear in mind

A most peculiar case, and straighten out

What's crooked there, before we close accounts.

Renounce the world for them—some day I will :

Meantime, to me let her become the world!"

Thus, mutely might our friend soliloquize

Over the tradesmen's bills, his Clara's gift—

In the apartment, Coliseum Street,

Carlino Centofanti's legacy,

Provided rent and taxes were discharged—

In face of Steiner now, De Millefleurs once,

The tailor's wife and runaway confessed.

On such a lady if election light,

(According to a social prejudice)

If henceforth "all the world" she constitute

For any lover,—needs must he renounce

Our world in ordinary, walked about

By couples loving as our laws prescribe,—

Renunciation sometimes difficult.

But, in this instance, time and place and thing

Combined to simplify experiment,

And make Miranda, in the current phrase,

Master the situation passably.

For first facility, his brother died—

Who was, I should have told you, confidant,

Adviser, referee and substitute,

All from a distance: but I knew how soon

This younger brother, lost in Portugal,

Had to depart and leave our friend at large.

Cut off abruptly from companionship

With brother-soul of bulk about as big,

(Obvious recipient—by intelligence

And sympathy, poor little pair of souls—

Of much affection and some foolishness)

Monsieur Léonce Miranda, meant to lean

By nature, needs must shift the leaning-place

To his love's bosom from his brother's neck,

Or fall flat unrelieved of freight sublime.

Next died the lord of the Aladdin's cave,

Master o' the mint and keeper of the keys

Of chests choakful with gold and silver changed

By Art to forms where wealth forgot itself,

And caskets where reposed each pullet-egg

Of diamond, slipping flame from fifty slants.

In short, the father of the family

Took his departure also from our scene,

Leaving a fat succession to his heir

Monsieur Léonce Miranda,—"fortunate

If ever man was, in a father's death,"

(So commented the world,—not he, too kind,

Could that be, rather than scarce kind enough)

Indisputably fortunate so far,

That little of incumbrance in his path,

Which money kicks aside, would lie there long.

And finally, a rough but wholesome shock,

An accident which comes to kill or cure,

A jerk which mends a dislocated joint !

Such happy chance, at cost of twinge, no doubt,

Into the socket back again put truth,

And stopped the limb from longer dragging lie.

For love suggested "Better shamble on,

·And bear your lameness with what grace you may !"

And but for this rude wholesome accident,

Continuance of disguise and subterfuge,

Retention of first falsehood as to name

And nature in the lady, might have proved

Too necessary for abandonment.

Monsieur Léonce Miranda probably

Had else been loath to cast the mask aside,

So politic, so self-preservative,

Therefore so pardonable—though so wrong !

For see the bugbear in the background !   Breathe

But ugly name, and wind is sure to waft

The husband news of the wife's whereabout :

From where he lies perdue in London town,

Forth steps the needy tailor on the stage,

Deity-like from dusk machine of fog,

And claims his consort, or his consort's worth   .

In rubies which her price is far above.

Hard to propitiate, harder to oppose,—

Who but the man's self came to banish fear,

A pleasant apparition, such as shocks

A moment, tells a tale, then goes for good!

Monsieur Ulysse Muhlhausen proved no less

Nor more than "Gustave," lodging opposite

Monsieur Léonce Miranda's diamond-cave

And ruby-mine, and lacking little thence

Save that its gnome would keep the captive safe,

Never return his Clara to his arms.

For why? . He was become the man in vogue,

The indispensable to who went clothed

Nor cared encounter Paris fashion's blame,—

Such miracle could London absencè work.

Rolling in riches—so translate " the vogue "—

Rather his object was to keep off claw

Should griffin scent the gold, should wife lay claim

To lawful portion at a future day,

Than tempt his partner from her private spoils.

Best forage each for each, nor coupled hunt !

Pursuantly, one morning,—knock at door

With knuckle, dry authoritative cough,

And easy stamp of foot, broke startlingly

On household slumber, Coliseum Street :

" Admittance in the name of Law !"   In marched

The Commissary and subordinate.

One glance sufficed them.   " A marital pair :

We certify, and bid good morning, sir !

Madame, a thousand pardons !"   Whereupon

Monsieur Ulysse Muhlhausen otherwise

Called "Gustave" for conveniency of trade,

Deposing in due form complaint of wrong,

Made his demand of remedy—divorce

From bed, board, share of name, and part in goods.

Monsieur Léonce Miranda owned his fault,

Protested his pure ignorance, from first

To last, of rights infringed in "Gustave's" case :

Submitted him to judgment. Law decreed

" Body and goods be henceforth separate ! "

And thereupon each party took its way,

This right, this left, rejoicing, to abide

Estranged yet amicable, opposites

In life as in respective dwelling-place.

Still does one read on his establishment

Huge-lettered " Gustave,"—gold out-glittering

"Miranda, goldsmith," just across the street—

"A first-rate hand at riding-habits"—say

The instructed—"special cut of chamber-robes."

Thus by a rude in seeming—rightlier judged

Beneficent surprise, publicity

Stopped further fear and trembling, and what tale

Cowardice thinks a covert : one bold splash

Into the mid-shame, and the shiver ends,

Though cramp and drowning may begin perhaps.

To cite just one more point which crowned success :

Madame, Miranda's mother, most of all

An obstacle to his projected life

In licence, as a daughter of the Church,

Duteous, exemplary, severe by right—

Moreover one most thoroughly beloved

Without a rival till the other sort

Possessed her son,—first storm of anger spent,

Seemed, grumblingly and grudgingly no doubt,

To acquiesce, let be what needs must be.

" With Heaven—accommodation possible !"

Saint Sganarelle had preached with such effect,

She saw now mitigating circumstance.

" The erring one was most unfortunate,

No question : but worse Magdalens repent.

Were Clara free, did only Law allow,

What fitter choice in marriage could have made

Léonce or anybody ? "   'Tis alleged

And evidenced, I find, by advocate

" Never did she consider such a tie

As baleful, springe to snap whate'er the cost."

K

And when the couple were in safety once

At Clairvaux, motherly, considerate,

She shrank not from advice. "Since safe you be,

Safely abide ! for Winter, I know well,

Is troublesome in a cold country-house.

I recommend the south room, that we styled,

Your sire and I, the Winter-chamber."

                                    Chance

Or purpose,—who can read the mystery ?—

Combined, I say, to bid " Entrench yourself,

Monsieur Léonce Miranda, on this turf,

About this flower, so firmly that, as tent

Rises on every side around you both,

The question shall become,—Which arrogates

Stability, the tent or towers afar ?

May not the temporary structure suit

The stable circuit, co-exist in peace ?—

Always until the proper time, no fear !

' Lay flat your tent ! ' is easier said than done."

So, with the best of auspices, betook

Themselves Léonce Miranda and his bride—

Provisionary—to their Clairvaux house,

Never to leave it—till the proper time.

I told you what was Clairvaux-Priory

Ere the improper time : an old demesne

With memories,—relic, half, and ruin, whole,—

The very place, then, to repair the wits

Worn out with Paris-traffic, when its lord,

Miranda's father took his month of ease

Purchased by industry.   What contrast here !

Repose, and solitude, and healthy ways !

That ticking at the back of head, he took

For motion of an inmate, stopped at once,

Proved nothing but the pavement's rattle left

Behind at Paris : here was holiday !

Welcome the quaint succeeding to the spruce,

The large and lumbersome and—might he breathe

In whisper to his own ear—dignified

And gentry-fashioned old-style haunts of sleep !

Palatial gloomy chambers for parade,

And passage-lengths of lost significance,

Never constructed as receptacle,

At his odd hours, for him their actual lord

By dint of diamond-dealing, goldsmithry.

Therefore Miranda's father chopped and changed

Nor roof-tile nor yet floor-brick, undismayed

By rains a-top or rats at bottom there.

Such contrast is so piquant for a month !

But now arrived quite other occupants

Whose cry was " Permanency,—life and death

Here, here, not elsewhere, change is all we dread !"

Their dwelling-place must be adapted, then,

To inmates, no mere truants from the town,

No temporary sojourners, forsooth,

At Clairvaux : change it into Paradise !

Fair friend,—who listen and let talk, alas !—

You would, in even such a state of things,

Pronounce,—or am I wrong ?—for bidding stay

The old-world inconvenience, fresh as found.

All folks of individuality

Prefer to be reminded, now and then,

Though at the cost of vulgar cosiness,

That the shell-outside only harbours man

The vital and progressive, meant to build,

When build he may, with quite a difference,

Some time, in that far land we dream about,

Where every man is his own architect.

But then the couple here in question, each

At one in project for a happy life,

Were by no acceptation of the word

So individual that they must aspire

To architecture all-appropriate

And, therefore, in this world impossible :

They needed house to suit the circumstance,

Proprietors, not tenants for a term.

Despite a certain marking, here and there,

Of fleecy black or white distinguishment,

These vulgar sheep wore the flock's uniform.

They love the country, *they* renounce the town?

They gave a kick, as our Italians say,

To Paris ere it turned and kicked themselves !

Acquaintances might prove too hard to seek,

Or the reverse of hard to find, perchance,

Since Monsieur Gustave's apparition there.

And let me call remark upon the list

Of notabilities invoked, in Court

At Vire, to witness, by their phrases culled

From correspondence, what was the esteem

Of those we pay respect to, for " the pair

Whereof they knew the inner life," 'tis said.

Three, and three only, answered the appeal.

First, Monsieur Vaillant, music-publisher,

" Begs Madame will accept civilities."

Next, Alexandre Dumas,—sire, not son,—

" Sends compliments to Madame and to you."

And last—but now prepare for England's voice !

I will not mar nor make—here's word for word—

" A rich proprietor of Paris, he

To whom belonged that beauteous *Bagatelle*

Close to the wood of Boulogne, Hertford hight,

Assures of homages and compliments

Affectionate "—not now Miranda but

" Madame Muhlhausen." (Was this friend, the Duke

Redoubtable in rivalry before ?)

Such was the evidence when evidence

Was wanted, then if ever, to the worth

Whereat acquaintances in Paris prized

Monsieur Léonce Miranda's household charm.

No wonder, then, his impulse was to live,

In Norman solitude, the Paris life :

Surround himself with Art transported thence,

And nature like those famed Elysian Fields :

Then, warm up the right colour out of both,

By Boulevard friendships tempted to come taste

How Paris lived again in little there.

Monsieur Léonce Miranda practised Art.

Do let a man for once live as man likes !

Politics ? Spend your life, to spare the world's :

Improve each unit by some particle

Of joy the more, deteriorate the orb

Entire, your own : poor profit, dismal loss !

Write books, paint pictures, or make music—since

Your nature leans to such life-exercise !

Ay, but such exercise begins too soon,

Concludes too late, demands life whole and sole,

Artistry being battle with the age

It lives in! Half life,—silence, while you learn

What has been done; the other half,—attempt

At speech, amid world's wail of wonderment—

" Here's something done, was never done before ! "

To be the very breath that moves the age,

Means not, to have breath drive you bubble-like

Before it—but yourself to blow: that's strain;

Strain 's worry through the life-time, till there's peace;

We know where peace expects the artist-soul.

Monsieur Léonce Miranda knew as much.

Therefore in Art he nowise cared to be

Creative ; but creation, that had birth

In storminess long years before was born

Monsieur Léonce Miranda,—Art, enjoyed

Like fleshly objects of the chace that tempt

In cookery, not capture—these might feast

The dilettante, furnish tavern-fare

Open to all with purses open too.

To sit free and take tribute seigneur-like—

Now, not too lavish of acknowledgment,

Now, self-indulgently profuse of pay,

Always Art's seigneur, not Art's serving-man,

Whate'er the style and title and degree,—

That is the quiet life and easy death

Monsieur Léonce Miranda would approve

Wholly—provided (back I go again

To the first simile) that while glasses clink,

And viands steam, and banqueting laughs high,

All that's outside the temporary tent,

The dim grim outline of the circuit-wall,

Forgets to menace "Soon or late will drop

Pavilion, soon or late you needs must march,

And laggards will be sorry they were slack!

Always—unless excuse sound plausible!"

Monsieur Léonce Miranda knew as much :

Whence his determination just to paint

So creditably as might help the eye

To comprehend how painter's eye grew dim

Ere it produced L'Ingegno's piece of work—

So to become musician that his ear

Should judge, by its own tickling and turmoil,

Who made the Solemn Mass might well die deaf—

So cultivate a literary knack

That, by experience how it wiles the time,

He might imagine how a poet, rapt

In rhyming wholly, grew so poor at last

By carelessness about his banker's-book,

That the Sieur Boileau (to provoke our smile)

Began abruptly,—when he paid devoir

To Louis Quatorze as he dined in state,—

"Sire, send a drop of broth to Pierre Corneille

Now dying and in want of sustenance !"

—I say, these half-hour playings at life's toil,

Diversified by billiards, riding, sport—

With now and then a visitor—Dumas,

Hertford—to check no aspiration's flight—

While Clara, like a diamond in the dark,

Should extract shining from what else were shade,

And multiply chance rays a million-fold,—

How could he doubt that all offence outside,—

Wrong to the towers, which, pillowed on the turf,

He thus shut eyes to,—were as good as gone?

So, down went Clairvaux-Priory to dust,

And up there rose, in lieu, yon structure gay

Above the Norman ghosts: and where the stretch

Of barren country girdled house about,

Behold the Park, the English preference!

Thus made undoubtedly a desert smile,

Monsieur Léonce Miranda.

       Ay, but she?

One should not so merge soul in soul, you think?

And I think: only, let us wait, nor want

Two things at once—her turn will come in time.

A cork-float danced upon the tide, we saw,

This morning, blinding-bright with briny dews :

There was no disengaging soaked from sound,

Earth-product from the sister-element.

But when we turn, the tide will turn, I think,

And bare on beach will lie exposed the buoy :

A very proper time to try, with foot

And even finger, which was buoying wave,

Which merely buoyant substance,—power to lift,

And power to be sent skyward passively.

Meanwhile, no separation of the pair !

III

And so slipt pleasantly away five years

Of Paradisiac dream; till, as there flit

Premonitory symptoms, pricks of pain,

Because the dreamer has to start awake

And find disease dwelt active all the while

In head or stomach through his night-long sleep,—

So happened here disturbance to content.

Monsieur Léonce Miranda's last of cares,

Ere he composed himself, had been to make

Provision that, while sleeping safe he lay,

Somebody else should, dragon-like, let fall

Never a lid, coiled round the apple-stem,

But watch the precious fruitage. Somebody

Kept shop, in short, played Paris substitute.

Himself, shrewd, well-trained, early-exercised,

Could take in, at an eye-glance, luck or loss—

Know commerce throve, though lazily uplift

On elbow merely : leave his bed, forsooth?

Such active service was the substitute's.

But one October morning, at first drop

Of appled gold, first summons to be grave

Because rough Autumn's play turns earnest now,

Monsieur Léonce Miranda was required

In Paris to take counsel, face to face,

With Madame-mother : and be rated, too,

L

Roundly at certain items of expense

Whereat the government provisional,

The Paris substitute and shopkeeper,

Shook head, and talked of funds inadequate :

Oh, in the long run,—not if remedy

Occurred betimes!   Else,—tap the generous bole

Too near the quick,—it withers to the root—

Leafy, prolific, golden apple-tree,

" Miranda," sturdy in the Place Vendôme !

" What is this reckless life you.lead ?" began

Madame Miranda,—whom he feared and loved,—

Her greeting.   " Luxury, extravagance

Sardanapalus' self might emulate,—

Did your good father's money go for this ?

Where are the fruits of education, where

The morals which at first distinguished you,

The faith which promised to adorn your age?

And why such wastefulness outbreaking now,

When heretofore you loved economy?

Explain this pulling-down and building up

Of Clairvaux, which your father bought because

Clairvaux he found it, and so left to you,

Not a gilt gingerbread big baby-house!

True, we could somehow shake head and shut eye

To what was past prevention on our part—

This reprehensible illicit bond:

We, in a manner, winking, watched consort

Our modest well-conducted pious son

With Dalilah: we thought the smoking flax

Would smoulder soon away and end in snuff!

Is spark to strengthen, prove consuming fire?

No lawful family calls Clairvaux ' home '—

Why play the fool of Scripture that the voice

Admonished 'Whose shall be those things to-night,

Provided for thy morning jollity?'

To take one specimen of pure caprice

Out of the heap conspicuous in this plan,—

Puzzle of change, I call it,—titled big

'Clairvaux Restored:' what means this Belvedere?

This Tower, stuck like a fools'-cap on the roof—

Do you intend to soar to heaven from thence?

Tower, truly! Better had you planted turf—

More fitly would you dig yourself a hole

Beneath it, for the final journey's help!

O we poor parents—could we prophesy!"

Léonce was found affectionate enough

To man, to woman, child, bird, beast, alike;

But all affection, all one fire of heart

Flaming toward Madame-mother.   Had she posed

The question plainly at the outset " Choose!

Cut clean in half your all-the-world of love,

The mother and the mistress: then resolve,

Take me or take her, throw away the one !"—

He might have made the choice and marred my tale.

But, much I apprehend, the problem put

Was " Keep both halves, yet do no detriment

To either!   Prize each opposite in turn!"

Hence, while he prized at worth the Clairvaux-life

With all its tolerated naughtiness,

He, visiting in fancy Quai Rousseau,

Saw, cornered in the cosiest nook of all

That range of rooms through number Thirty-three,

The lady-mother bent o'er her *Bézique;*

While Monsieur Curé This, and Sister That,—

Superior of no matter what good House—

Did duty for Duke Hertford and Dumas,

Nay,—at his mother's age,—for Clara's self.

At Quai Rousseau, things comfortable thus,

Why should poor Clairvaux be so troublesome?

She played at cards, he built a Belvedere.

But here's the difference : she had reached the Towers

And there took pastime : he was still on Turf—

Though fully minded that, when once he marched,

* No sportive fancy should distract him more.

In brief, the man was angry with himself,

With her, with all the world and much beside :

And so the unseemly words were interchanged

Which crystalize what else evaporates,

And make mere misty petulance grow hard

And sharp inside each softness, heart and soul.

Monsieur Léonce Miranda flung at last

Out of doors, fever-flushed : and there the Seine

Rolled at his feet, obsequious remedy

For fever, in a cold Autumnal flow.

" Go and be rid of memory in a bath ! "

Craftily whispered Who besets the ear

On such occasions.

      Done as soon as dreamed.

Back shivers poor Léonce to bed—where else ?

And there he lies a month 'twixt life and death,

Raving. " Remorse of conscience ! " friends

 opine.

" Sirs, it may partly prove so," represents

Beaumont—(the family physician, he

Whom last year's Commune murdered, do you mind?)

Beaumont reports " There is some active cause,

More than mere pungency of quarrel past,—

Cause that keeps adding other food to fire.

I hear the words and know the signs, I say !

Dear Madame, you have read the Book of Saints,

How Antony was tempted ?   As for me,

Poor heathen, 'tis by pictures I am taught.

I say then, I see standing here,—between

Me and my patient, and that crucifix

You very properly would interpose,—

A certain woman-shape, one white appeal

' Will you leave me, then, me, me, me for her?'

Since cold Seine could not quench this flame, since flare

Of fever does not redden it away,—

Be rational, indulgent, mute—should chance

Come to the rescue—Providence, I mean—

The while I blister and phlebotomize!"

Well, somehow rescued by whatever power,

At month's end, back again conveyed himself

Monsieur Léonce Miranda, worn to rags,

Nay, tinder: stuff irreparably spoiled,

Though kindly hand should stitch and patch its
      best.

Clairvaux in Autumn is restorative.

A friend stitched on, patched ever. All the same,

Clairvaux looked greyer than a month ago.

Unglossed was shrubbery, unglorified

Each copse, so wealthy once; the garden-plots,

The orchard-walks showed dearth and dreariness.

The sea lay out at distance crammed by cloud

Into a leaden wedge; and sorrowful

Sulked field and pasture with persistent rain.

Nobody came so far from Paris now:

Friends did their duty by an invalid

Whose convalescence claimed entire repose.

Only a single ministrant was staunch

At quiet reparation of the stuff—

Monsieur Léonce Miranda, worn to rags:

But she was Clara and the world beside.

Another month, the year packed up his plagues

And sullenly departed, pedlar-like,

As apprehensive old-world ware might show

To disadvantage when the new-comer,

Merchant of novelties, young 'Sixty-eight,

With bran-new bargains, whistled o'er the lea.

Things brightened somewhat o'er the Christmas hearth,

As Clara plied assiduously her task.

" Words are but words and wind.   Why let the wind

Sing in your ear, bite, sounding, to your brain ?

Old folk and young folk, still at odds, of course !

Age quarrels because Spring puts forth a leaf

While Winter has a mind that boughs stay bare ;

Or rather—worse than quarrel—age descries

Propriety in preaching life to death.

' Enjoy nor youth, nor Clairvaux, nor poor me ? '

Dear Madame, you enjoy your age, 'tis thought !

Your number Thirty-three on Quai Rousseau

Cost fifty times the price of Clairvaux, tipped

Even with our prodigious Belvedere ;

You entertain the Curé,—we, Dumas :

We play charades, while you prefer *Bézique :*

Do lead your own life and let ours alone !

Cross Old Year shall have done his worst, my

    friend !

Here comes gay New Year with a gift, no doubt !

Look up and let in light that longs to shine—

One flash of light, and where will darkness hide ?

Your cold makes me too cold, love ! Keep me warm !"

Whereat Léonce Miranda raised his head

From his two white thin hands, and forced a smile,

And spoke : "I do look up, and see your light

Above me ! Let New Year contribute warmth—

I shall refuse no fuel that may blaze."

Nor did he.   Three days after, just a spark

From Paris, answered by a snap at Caen

Or whither reached the telegraphic wire:

"Quickly to Paris!   On arrival, learn

Why you are wanted!"   Curt and critical!

Off starts Léonce, one fear from head to foot;

Caen, Rouen, Paris, as the railway helps;

Then come the Quai and Number Thirty-three.

"What is the matter, concierge?"—a grimace!

He mounts the staircase, makes for the main seat

Of dreadful mystery which draws him there—

Bursts in upon a bedroom known too well—

There lies all left now of the mother once.

Tapers define the stretch of rigid white,

Nor want there ghastly velvets of the grave.

A blackness sits on either side at watch,

Sisters, good souls but frightful all the same,

Silent : a priest is spokesman for his corpse.

" Dead, through Léonce Miranda ! stricken down

Without a minute's warning, yesterday!

What did she say to you, and you to her,

Two months ago?   This is the consequence !

The doctors have their name for the disease ;

I, you, and God say—heart-break, nothing more !"

Monsieur Léonce Miranda, like a stone

Fell at the bedfoot and found respite so,

While the priest went to tell the company.

What follows you are free to disbelieve.

It may be true or false that this good priest

Had taken his instructions,—who shall blame ?—

From quite another quarter than, perchance,

Monsieur Léonce Miranda might suppose

Would offer solace in such pressing need.

All he remembered of his kith and kin

Was, they were worthily his substitutes

In commerce, did their work and drew their pay.

But *they* remembered, in addition, this—

They fairly might expect inheritance,

As nearest kin, called Family by law

And gospel both.   Now, since Miranda's life

Showed nothing like abatement of distaste

For conjugality, but preference

Continued and confirmed of that smooth chain

Which slips and leaves no knot behind, no heir—

Presumption was, the man, become mature,

Would at a calculable day, discard

His old and outworn . . what we blush to name,

And make society the just amends;

Scarce by a new attachment—Heaven forbid!

Still less by lawful marriage: that's reserved

For those who make a proper choice at first—

Not try both courses and would grasp in age

The very treasure, youth preferred to spurn!

No! putting decently such thought aside,

The penitent must rather give his powers

To such a reparation of the past

As, edifying kindred, makes them rich.

Now, how would it enrich prospectively

The Cousins, if he lavished such expense

On Clairvaux?—pretty as a toy, but then

As toy, so much productive, and no more!

If all the outcome of the goldsmith's shop

Went to gild Clairvaux, where remained the funds

For Cousinry to spread out lap and take ?

This must be thought of and provided for !

I give it you as mere conjecture, mind !

To help explain the wholesome unannounced

Intelligence, the shock that startled guilt,

The scenic show, much yellow, black and white

By taper-shine, the nuns—portentous pair,

And, more than all, the priest's admonishment—

" No flattery of self !   You murdered her !

The grey lips, silent now, reprove by mine.

You wasted all your living, rioted

In harlotry—she warned and I repeat !

No warning had she, for she needed none :

If this should be the last yourself receive ? "

Done for the best, no doubt, though clumsily,—

Such, and so startling, the reception here,

M

You hardly wonder if down fell at once

The tawdry tent, pictorial, musical,

Poetical, besprent with hearts and darts ;

Its cobweb-work, betinseled stitchery,

Lay dust about our sleeper on the turf,

And showed an outer wall distinct and dread.

Senseless he fell, and long he lay, and much

Seemed salutary in his punishment

To planners and performers of the piece.

When pain ends, pardon prompt may operate.

There was a good attendance close at hand,

Waiting the issue in the great saloon,

Cousins with consolation and advice.

All things thus happily performed to point,

No wonder at success commensurate.

Once swooning stopped, once anguish subsequent

Raved out,—a sudden resolution chilled

His blood and changed his swimming eyes to stone,

As the poor fellow raised himself upright,

Collected strength, looked, once for all, his look,

Then, turning, put officious help aside

And passed from out the chamber. " For affairs ! "

So he announced himself to the saloon :

" We owe a duty to the living too ! "—

Monsieur Léonce Miranda tried to smile.

How did the hearts of Cousinry rejoice

At their stray sheep returning thus to fold,

As, with a dignity, precision, sense,

All unsuspected in the man before,

Monsieur Léonce Miranda made minute

Detail of his intended scheme of life

Thenceforward and for ever.   "Vanity

Was ended : its redemption must begin—

And, certain, would continue ; but since life

Was awfully uncertain—witness here !—

Behoved him lose no moment, but discharge

Immediate burthen of the world's affairs

On backs that kindly volunteered to crouch.

Cousins, with easier conscience, blamelessly

Might carry on the goldsmith's trade, in brief,

Uninterfered with by its lord who late

Was used to supervise and take due tithe.

A stipend now sufficed his natural need :

Themselves should fix what sum allows man live.

But half a dozen words concisely plain

Might, first of all, make sure that, on demise,

Monsieur Léonce Miranda's property

Passed by bequeathment, every particle,

To the right heirs, the cousins of his heart.

As for that woman—they would understand!

This was a step would take her by surprise!

It were too cruel did he snatch away

Decent subsistence.   She was young, and fair,

And . . and attractive!   Means must be supplied

To save her from herself, and from the world,

And . . from anxieties, might haunt him else

When he were fain have other thoughts in mind."

It was a sight to melt a stone, that thaw

Of rigid disapproval into dew

Of sympathy, as each extended palm

Of cousin hasted to enclose those five

Cold fingers, tendered so mistrustfully,

Despairingly of condonation now !

One would have thought,—at every fervent shake,

In reassurance of those timid tips,—

The penitent had squeezed, considerate,

By way of fee into physician's hand

For physicking his soul, some diamond knob.

And now let pass a week.   Once more behold

The same assemblage in the same saloon—

Waiting the entry of protagonist

Monsieur Léonce Miranda.   " Just a week

Since the death-day,—was ever man transformed

Like this man ? " questioned cousin of his mate.

Last seal to the repentance had been set

Three days before, at Sceaux in neighbourhood

Of Paris, where they laid with funeral pomp

Mother by father.   Let me spare the rest:

How the poor fellow, in his misery,

Buried hot face and bosom, where heaped snow

Offered assistance, at the grave's black edge,

And there lay, till uprooted by main force

From where he prayed to grow and ne'er again

Walk earth unworthily as heretofore.

It is not with impunity priests teach

The doctrine he was dosed with from his youth—

" Pain to the body—profit to the soul ;

Corporeal pleasure—so much woe to pay

When disembodied spirit gives account."

However, woe had done its worst, this time.

Three days allow subsidence of much grief.

Already, regular and equable,

Forward went purpose to effect.   At once

The testament was written, signed and sealed.

Disposure of the commerce—that took time,

And would not suffer by a week's delay ;

But the immediate, the imperious need,

The call demanding of the Cousinry

Co-operation, what convened them thus,

Was—how and when should deputation march

To Coliseum Street, the old abode

Of wickedness, and there acquaint—oh, shame!

Her, its old inmate, who had followed up

And lay in wait in the old haunt for prey—

That they had rescued, they possessed Léonce,

Whose loathing at re-capture equalled theirs—

Upbraid that sinner with her sinfulness,

Impart the fellow-sinner's firm resolve

Never to set eyes on her face again :

Then, after stipulations strict but just,

Hand her the first instalment,—moderate

Enough, no question,—of her salary :

Admonish for the future, and so end.—

All which good purposes, decided on

Sufficiently, were waiting full effect

When presently the culprit should appear.

Somehow appearance was delayed too long;

Chatting and chirping sunk inconsciously

To silence, nay, uneasiness, at length

Alarm, till—anything for certitude !—

A peeper was commissioned to explore,

At keyhole, what the laggard's task might be—

What caused so palpable a disrespect!

Back came the tiptoe cousin from his quest.

" Monsieur Léonce was busy," he believed,

" Contemplating—those love-letters, perhaps,

He always carried, as if precious stones,

About with him.   He read, one after one,

Some sort of letters.   But his back was turned.

The empty coffer open at his side,

He leant on elbow by the mantelpiece

Before the hearth-fire ; big and blazing too."

" Better he shovelled them all in at once,

And burned the rubbish!" was a cousin's quip,

Warming his own hands at the fire the while.

I told you, snow had fallen outside, I think.

When suddenly a cry, a host of cries,

Screams, hubbub and confusion thrilled the room.

All by a common impulse rushed thence, reached

The late death-chamber, tricked with trappings still,

Skulls, cross-bones, and such moral broidery.

Madame Muhlhausen might have played the witch,

Dropped down the chimney and appalled Léonce

By some proposal " Parting touch of hand ! "

If she but touched his foolish hand, you know ! !

Something had happened quite contrariwise.

Monsieur Léonce Miranda, one by one,

Had read the letters and the love they held,

And that task finished, had required his soul

To answer frankly what the prospect seemed

Of his own love's departure—pledged to part!

Then, answer being unmistakable,

He had replaced the letters quietly,

Shut coffer, and so, grasping either side

By its convenient handle, plunged the whole—

Letters and coffer and both hands to boot,

Into the burning grate and held them there.

" Burn, burn and purify my past!" said he,

Calmly, as if he felt no pain at all.

In vain they pulled him from the torture-place :

The strong man, with the soul of tenfold strength,

Broke from their clutch : and there again smiled he,

The miserable hands re-bathed in fire—

Constant to that ejaculation " Burn,

Burn, purify ! "   And when, combining force,

They fairly dragged the victim out of reach

Of further harm, he had no hands to hurt—

Two horrible remains of right and left,

" Whereof the bones, phalanges formerly,

Carbonised, were still crackling with the flame,"

Said Beaumont.   And he fought them all the while :

" Why am I hindered when I would be pure ?

Why leave the sacrifice still incomplete ?

She holds me, I must have more hands to burn ! "

They were the stronger, though, and bound him
  fast.

Beaumont was in attendance presently.

" What did I tell you ?   Preachment to the deaf !

I wish he had been deafer when they preached,

Those priests!   But wait till next Republic comes!"

As for Léonce, a single sentiment

Possessed his soul and occupied his tongue—

Absolute satisfaction at the deed.

Never he varied, 'tis observable,

Nor in the stage of agonies (which proved

Absent without leave,—science seemed to think)

Nor yet in those three months' febricity

Which followed,—never did he vary tale—

Remaining happy beyond utterance.

" Ineffable beatitude "—I quote

The words, I cannot give the smile—" such bliss

Abolished pain ! Pain might or might not be :

He felt in heaven, where flesh desists to fret.

Purified now and henceforth, all the past

Reduced to ashes with the flesh defiled!

Why all those anxious faces round his bed?

What was to pity in their patient, pray,

When doctor came and went, and Cousins watched?

—Kindness, but in pure waste!" he said and smiled.

And if a trouble would at times disturb

The ambrosial mood, it came from other source

Than the corporeal transitory pang.

"If sacrifice be incomplete!" cried he—

"If ashes have not sunk reduced to dust,

To nullity! If atoms coälesce

Till something grow, grow, get to be a shape

I hate, I hoped to burn away from me!

She is my body, she and I are one,

Yet, all the same, there, there at bed-foot stands

The woman wound about my flesh and blood,

There, the arms open, the more wonderful,

The whiter for the burning . . Vanish thou!

Avaunt, fiend's self found in the form I wore!"

"Whereat," said Beaumont, "since his hands were gone,

The patient in a frenzy kicked and kicked

To keep off some imagined visitant.

So will it prove as long as priests may preach

Spiritual terrors!" groaned the evidence

Of Beaumont that his patient was stark mad—

Produced in time and place: of which anon.

"Mad, or why thus insensible to pain?

Body and soul are one thing, with two names

For more or less elaborated stuff."

Such is the new *Religio Medici*.

Though antiquated faith held otherwise,

Explained that body is not soul, but just

Soul's servant : that, if soul be satisfied,

Possess already joy or pain enough,

It uses to ignore, as master may,

What increase, joy or pain, its servant brings—

Superfluous contribution : soul, once served,

Has nought to do with body's service more.

Each, speculated on exclusively,

As if its office were the only one,

Body or soul, shows either, service paid

In joy and pain, that's blind and objectless—

A servant toiling for no master's good—

Or else shows good received and put to use,

As if within soul's self grew joy and pain,

N

Nor needed body for a ministrant.

I note these old unscientific ways :

Poor Beaumont cannot: for the Commune ruled

Next year, and ere they shot his priests, shot him.

Monsieur Léonce Miranda raved himself

To rest ; lay three long months in bliss or bale,

Inactive, anyhow : more need that heirs,

His natural protectors, should assume

The management, bestir their cousinship,

And carry out that purpose of reform

Such tragic work now made imperative.

A deputation, with austerity,

Nay, sternness, bore her sentence to the fiend

Aforesaid,—she at watch for turn of wheel

And fortune's favour, Street—you know the name.

A certain roughness seemed appropriate : " You—

Steiner, Muhlhausen, whatsoe'er your name,

Cause whole and sole of this catastrophe! "—

And so forth, introduced the embassage.

" Monsieur Léonce Miranda was divorced

Once and for ever from his—ugly word.

Himself had gone for good to Portugal :

They came empowered to act and stipulate.

Hold ! no discussion !   Terms were settled now :

So much of present and prospective pay,

But also—good engagement in plain terms

She never seek renewal of the past ! "

This little harmless tale produced effect.

Madame Muhlhausen owned her sentence just,

Its execution gentle.   "Stern their phrase,

These kinsfolk with a right she recognised—

But kind its import probably, which now

Her agitation, her bewilderment,

Rendered too hard to understand, perhaps.

Let them accord the natural delay,

And she would ponder and decide.   Meantime,

So far was she from wish to follow friend

Who fled her, that she would not budge from place—

Now that her friend was fled to Portugal,—

Never! *She* leave this Coliseum Street?

No, not a footstep!" she assured them.

                              So—

They saw they might have left that tale untold

When, after some weeks more were gone to waste,

Recovery seemed incontestable,

And the poor mutilated figure, once

The gay and glancing fortunate young spark,

Miranda, humble and obedient took

The doctor's counsel, issued sad and slow

From precincts of the sick-room, tottered down,

And out, and into carriage for fresh air,

And so drove straight to Coliseum Street,

And tottered upstairs, knocked, and in a trice

Was clasped in the embrace of whom you know—

With much asseveration, I omit,

Of constancy henceforth till life should end.

When all this happened,—"What reward," cried she,

" For judging her Miranda by herself !

For never having entertained a thought

Of breaking promise, leaving home forsooth,

To follow who was fled to Portugal !

As if she thought they spoke a word of truth !

She knew what love was, knew that he loved her ;

The Cousinry knew nothing of the kind."

I will not scandalize you and recount

How matters made the morning pass away.

Not one reproach, not one acknowledgment,

One explanation: all was understood !

Matters at end, the home-uneasiness

Cousins were feeling at this jaunt prolonged

Was ended also by the entry of—

Not simply him whose exit had been made

By mild command of doctor " Out with you !

I warrant we receive another man !"

But—would that I could say, the married pair !

And, quite another man assuredly,

Monsieur Léonce Miranda took on him

Forthwith to bid the trio, priest and nuns,

Constant in their attendance all this while,

Take his thanks and their own departure too;

Politely but emphatically.   Next,

The Cousins were dismissed: "No protest, pray!

Whatever I engaged to do is done,

Or shall be—I but follow your advice:

Love I abjure: the lady, you behold,

Is changed as I myself; her sex is changed:

This is my Brother—He will tend me now,

Be all my world henceforth as brother should.

Gentlemen, of a kinship I revere,

Your interest in trade is laudable;

I purpose to indulge it: manage mine,

My goldsmith-business in the Place Vendôme,

Wholly—through purchase at the price adjudged

By experts I shall have assistance from.

If, in conformity with sage advice,

I leave a busy world of interests

I own myself unfit for—yours the care

That any world of other aims, wherein

I hope to dwell, be easy of access

Through ministration of the moneys due,

As we determine, with all proper speed,

Since I leave Paris to repair my health.

Say farewell to our Cousins, Brother mine ! "

And, all submissiveness, as brother might,

The lady curtseyed gracefully, and dropt

More than mere curtsey, a concluding phrase

So silver-soft, yet penetrative too,

That none of it escaped the favoured ears :

" Had I but credited one syllable,

I should to-day be lying stretched on straw,

The produce of your miserable *rente* !

Whereas, I hold him—do you comprehend ? "

Cousin regarded cousin, turned up eye,

And took departure, as our Tuscans laugh,

Each with his added palm-breadth of long nose,—

Curtailed but imperceptibly, next week,

When transfer was accomplished, and the trade

In Paris did indeed become their own,

But bought by them and sold by him on terms

'Twixt man and man,—might serve 'twixt wolf and wolf,

Substitute " bit and clawed " for " signed and sealed "—

Our ordinary business-terms, in short.

Another week, and Clairvaux broke in bloom

At end of April, to receive again

Monsieur Léonce Miranda, gentleman,

Ex-jeweller and goldsmith : never more,—

According to the purpose he professed,—

To quit this paradise, his property,

This Clara, his companion: so it proved.

The Cousins, each with elongated nose,

Discussed their bargain, reconciled them soon

To hard necessity, disbursed the cash,

And hastened to subjoin, wherever type

Proclaimed " Miranda " to the public, " Called

Now Firm-Miranda". There, a colony,

They flourish underneath the name that still

Maintains the old repute, I understand.

They built their Clairvaux, dream-Château, in Spain,

Perhaps—but Place Vendôme is waking worth :

Oh, they lost little!—only, man and man

Hardly conclude transactions of the kind

As cousin should with cousin,—cousins think.

For the rest, all was honorably done,

So, ere buds break to blossom, let us breathe !

Never suppose there was one particle

Of recrudescence—wound, half-healed before,

Set freshly running—sin, repressed as such,

New loosened as necessity of life !

In all this revocation and resolve,

Far be sin's self-indulgence from your thought !

The man had simply made discovery,

By process I respect if not admire,

That what was, was :—that turf, his feet had touched,

Felt solid just as much as yonder wall

He saw with eyes, but did not stand upon,

And could not, if he would, reach in a leap.

People had told him flowery turf was false

To footstep, tired the traveller soon, beside :

That was untrue.   They told him " One fair stride

Plants on safe platform and secures man rest."

That was untrue.   Some varied the advice :

" Neither was solid, towers no more than turf"

Double assertion, therefore twice as false.

" I like these amateurs "—our friend had laughed

Could he turn what he felt to what he thought,

And, that again, to what he put in words :

" I like their pretty trial, proof of paste

Or precious stone, by delicate approach

Of eye askance, fine feel of finger-tip,

Or touch of tongue inquisitive for cold.

I tried my jewels in a crucible:

Fierce fire has felt them, licked them, left them sound.

Don't tell me that my earthly love is sham,

My heavenly fear a clever counterfeit!

Each may oppose each, yet be true alike!"

To build up, independent of the towers,

A durable pavilion o'er the turf,

Had issued in disaster. "What remained

Except, by tunnel, or else gallery,

To keep communication 'twixt the two,

Unite the opposites, both near and far,

And never try complete abandonment

Of one or other?" so he thought, not said.

And to such engineering feat, I say,

Monsieur Léonce Miranda saw the means

Precisely in this revocation prompt

Of just those benefits of worldly wealth

Conferred upon his Cousinry—all but !

This Clairvaux—you would know, were you at top

Of yonder crowning grace, its Belvedere—

Is situate in one angle-niche of three,

At equidistance from Saint-Rambert—there

Behind you, and The Ravissante, beside—

There : steeple, steeple, and this Clairvaux-top,

(A sort of steeple) constitute a trine,

With not a tenement to break each side,

Two miles or so in length, if eye can judge.

Now, this is native land of miracle.

O why, why, why, from all recorded time,

Was miracle not wrought, but only once,

To help whoever wanted help indeed?

If on the day when Spring's green girlishness

Grew nubile and she trembled into May,

And our Miranda climbed to clasp the Spring

A-tiptoe o'er the sea, those wafts of warmth,

Those cloudlets scudding under the bare blue,

And all that new sun, that fresh hope about

His airy place of observation,—friend,

Feel with me that if just then, just for once,

Some angel,—such as the authentic pen

Yonder records a daily visitant

Of ploughman Claude, rheumatic in the joints,

And spinster Jeanne, with megrim troubled much,—

If such an angel, with nought else to do,

Had taken station on the pinnacle

And simply said " Léonce, look straight before !

Neither to right hand nor to left : for why ?

Being a stupid soul, you want a guide

To turn the goodness in you to account

And make stupidity submit itself.

Go to Saint-Rambert !   Straightway get such guide !

There stands a man of men.   You, jeweller,

Must needs have heard how once the biggest block

Of diamond now in Europe lay exposed

Mid specimens of stone and earth and ore,

On huckster's stall,—Navona names the Square,

And Rome the city for the incident,—

Labelled ' quartz-crystal, price one halfpenny.'

Haste and secure that ha'p'worth, on your life !

That man will read you rightly head to foot,

Mark the brown face of you, the bushy beard,

The breadth 'twixt shoulderblades, and through each black

Castilian orbit, see into your soul.

Talk to him for five minutes—nonsense, sense,

No matter what—describe your horse, your hound,—

Give your opinion of the policy

Of Monsieur Rouher,—will he succour Rome?

Your estimate of what may outcome be

From Œcumenical Assemblage there!

After which samples of intelligence,

Rapidly run through those events you call

Your past life, tell what once you tried to do,

What you intend on doing this next May!

There he stands, reads an English newspaper,

Stock-still, and now, again upon the move,

o

Paces the beach to taste the Spring, like you,

Since both are human beings in God's eye.

He will have understood you, I engage.

Endeavour, for your part, to understand

He knows more, and loves better, than the world

That never heard his name, and never may.

He will have recognised, ere breath be spent

And speech at end, how much that's good in man,

And generous, and self-devoting, makes

Monsieur Léonce Miranda worth his help ;

While sounding to the bottom ignorance

Historical and philosophical

And moral and religious, all one couch

Of crassitude, a portent of its kind.

Then, just as he would pityingly teach

Your body to repair maltreatment, give

Advice that you should make those stumps to stir

With artificial hands of caoutchouc,

So would he soon supply your crippled soul

With crutches, from his own intelligence,

Able to help you onward in the path

Of rectitude whereto your face is set,

And counsel justice—to yourself, the first,

To your associate, very like a wife

Or something better,—to the world at large,

Friends, strangers, horses, hounds and Cousinry—

All which amount of justice will include

Justice to God.   Go and consult his voice !"

Since angel would not say this simple truth,

What hinders that my heart relieve itself,

O friend, who makest warm my wintry world,

And wise my heaven, if there we consort too?

Monsieur Léonce Miranda turned, alas,

Or was turned, by no angel, t'other way,

And got him guidance of The Ravissante.

Now, into the originals of faith,

Yours, mine, Miranda's, no enquiry here !

Of faith, as apprehended by mankind,

The causes, were they caught and catalogued,

Would too distract, too desperately foil

Enquirer.   How may analyst reduce

Quantities to exact their opposites,

Value to zero, then bring zero back

To value of supreme preponderance ?

How substitute thing meant for thing expressed ?

Detect the wire-thread through that fluffy silk

Men call their rope, their real compulsive power ?

Suppose effected such anatomy,

And demonstration made of what belief

Has moved believer—were the consequence

Reward at all? would each man straight deduce,

From proved reality of cause, effect

Conformable? believe and unbelieve

According to your True thus disengaged

From all his heap of False called reason first?

No: hand once used to hold a soft thick twist,

Cannot now grope its way by wire alone:

Childhood may catch the knack, scarce Youth, not Age!

That's the reply rewards you. Just as well

Remonstrate to yon peasant in the blouse

That, had he justified the true intent

Of Nature who composed him thus and thus,

Weakly or strongly, here he would not stand

Struggling with uncongenial earth and sky,

But elsewhere tread the surface of the globe,

Since one meridian suits the faulty lungs,

Another bids the sluggish liver work.

" Here I was born, for better or for worse :

I did not choose a climate for myself ;

Admit, my life were healthy, led elsewhere,"

(He answers) " how am I to migrate, pray ? "

Therefore the course to take is—spare your pains,

And trouble uselessly with discontent

Nor soul nor body, by parading proof

That neither haply had known ailment, placed

Precisely where the circumstance forbade

Their lot should fall to either of the pair.

But try and, what you find wrong, remedy,

Accepting the conditions : never ask

" How came you to be born here with those

     lungs,

That liver ? " But bid asthma smoke a pipe,

Stramonium, just as if no Tropics were,

And ply with calomel the sluggish duct,

Nor taunt " The born Norwegian breeds no bile ! "

And as with body, so proceed with soul :

Nor less discerningly, where faith you found,

However foolish and fantastic, grudge

To play the doctor and amend mistake,

Because a wisdom were conceivable

Whence faith had sprung robust above disease.

Far beyond human help, that source of things !

Since, in the first stage, so to speak,—first stare

Of apprehension at the invisible,

Begins divergency of mind from mind,

Superior from inferior : leave this first !

Little you change there !   What comes afterward—

From apprehended thing, each inference

With practicality concerning life,

This you may test and try, confirm the right

Or contravene the wrong which reasons there.

The offspring of the sickly faith must prove

Sickly act also : stop a monster-birth !

When water's in the cup and not the cloud,

Then is the proper time for chemic test :

Belief permits your skill to operate

When, drop by drop condensed from misty heaven,

'Tis wrung out, lies a bowl-full in the fleece.

How dew came down to earth, let Gideon say :

What purpose water serves, your word or two

May teach him, should he fancy it lights fire.

Concerning, then, our vaporous Ravissante—

How fable first precipitated faith—

Silence you get upon such point from me.

But when I see come posting to the pair

At Clairvaux, for the cure of soul-disease,

This Father of the Mission, Parish-priest,

· This Mother of the Convent, Nun I know—

They practise in that second stage of things ;

They boast no fresh distillery of faith ;

'Tis dogma in the bottle, bright and old,

They bring ; and I pretend to pharmacy.

They undertake the cure with all my heart !

He trusts them, and they surely trust themselves.

I ask no better.   Never mind the cause,

Fons et origo of the malady,

Apply the drug with courage!   Here's our

   case.

Monsieur Léonce Miranda asks of God,

—May a man, living in illicit tie,

Continue, by connivance of the Church,

No matter what amends he please to make

Short of forthwith relinquishing the sin?

Physicians, what do you propose for cure?

Father and Mother of the Ravissante,

Read your own records, and you find prescribed

As follows, when a couple out of sorts

Rather than gravely suffering, sought your skill

And thereby got their health again.   Perpend!

Two and a half good centuries ago,

Luc de la Maison Rouge, a nobleman

Of Claise, (the river gives this country name)

And, just as noblewoman, Maude his wife,

Having been married many happy years

Spent in God's honor and man's service too,

Conceived, while yet in flower of youth and hope,

The project of departing each from each

Forever, and dissolving marriage-bonds

That both might enter a religious life.

Needing, before they came to such resolve,

Divine illumination,—course was clear,—

They visited your church in pilgrimage.

On Christmas morn, communicating straight,

They heard three Masses proper for the day,

" It is incredible with what effect "—

Quoth the Cistercian monk I copy from—

And, next day, came, again communicants,

Again heàrd Masses manifold, but now

With added thanks to Christ for special grace

And consolation granted : in the night,

Had been divorce from marriage, manifest

By signs and tokens.   So, they made great gifts,

Left money for more Masses, and returned

Homeward rejoicing—he, to take the rules,

As Brother Dionysius, Capucin,

She, to become first postulant, then nun

According to the rules of Benedict,

Sister Scolastica : so ended they,

And so do I—not end nor yet commence

One note or comment.   What was done was

    done.

Now, Father of the Mission, here's your case!

And, Mother of the Convent, here's its cure!

If separation was permissible,

And that decree of Christ " What God hath joined

Let no man put asunder" nullified

Because a couple, blameless in the world,

Had the conceit that, still more blamelessly,

Out of the world, by breach of marriage-vow,

Their life was like to pass,—you oracles

Of God,—since holy Paul says such you are,—

Hesitate, not one moment, to pronounce

When questioned by the pair now needing help

" Each from the other go, you guilty ones,

Preliminary to your least approach

Nearer the Power that thus could strain a point

In favour of a pair of innocents

Who thought their wedded hands not clean enough

To touch and leave unsullied their souls' snow !

Are not your hands found filthy by the world,

Mere human law and custom ?   Not a step

Nearer till hands be washed and purified!"

What they did say is immaterial, since

Certainly it was nothing of the kind.

There was no washing hands of him (alack,

You take me ?—in the figurative sense !)

But, somehow, gloves were drawn o'er dirt and all,

And practice with the Church procured thereby.

Seeing that,—all remonstrance proved in vain,

Persuasives tried and terrors put to use,

I nowise question,—when the guilty pair

Only embraced the closelier, obstinate,—

Father and Mother went from Clairvaux back

Their weary way, with heaviness of heart,

I grant you, but each palm well crossed with coin,

And nothing like a smutch perceptible.

Monsieur Léonce Miranda might compound

For sin ?—no, surely ! but by gifts—prepare

His soul the better for contrition, say !

Gift followed upon gift, at all events.

Good counsel was rejected, on one part :

Hard money, on the other—may we hope

Was unreflectingly consigned to purse ?

Two years did this experiment engage

Monsieur Léonce Miranda : how by gifts

To God and to God's poor, a man might stay

In sin and yet stave off sin's punishment.

No salve could be conceived more nicely mixed

For this man's nature : generosity,—

Susceptibility to human ills,

Corporeal, mental,—self-devotedness

Made up Miranda—whether strong or weak

Elsewhere, may be enquired another time.

In mercy, he was strong, at all events.

Enough ! he could not see a beast in pain,

Much less a man, without the will to aid ;

And where the will was, there the means were too,

Since that good bargain with the Cousinry.

The news flew fast about the countryside

That, with the kind man, it was ask and have ;

And ask and have they did.   To instance you :—

A mob of beggars at The Ravissante

Clung to his skirts one day, and cried " We thirst ! "

Forthwith he bade a cask of wine be broached

To satisfy all comers, till, dead-drunk

And satisfied, they strewed the holy place.

For this was grown religious and a rite:

Such slips of judgment, gifts irregular,

Showed but as spillings of the golden grist

On either side the hopper, through blind zeal;

Steadily the main stream went pouring on

From mill to mouth of sack—held wide and close

By Father of the Mission, Parish-priest,

And Mother of the Convent, Nun I know,

With such effect that, in the sequel, proof

Was tendered to the Court at Vire, last month,

That in these same two years, expenditure

At quiet Clairvaux rose to the amount

Of Forty Thousand English pounds : whereof

A trifle went, no inappropriate close

Of bounty, to supply the Virgin's crown

With that stupendous jewel from New-York,

Now blazing as befits the Star of Sea.

Such signs of grace, outward and visible,

I rather give you, for your sake and mine,

Than put in evidence the inward strife,

Spiritual effort to compound for fault

By payment of devotion—thank the phrase !

That payment was as punctual, do not doubt,

As its far easier fellow.   Yesterday

I trudged the distance from The Ravissante

To Clairvaux, with my two feet : but our friend,

The more to edify the country-folk,

Was wont to make that journey on both knees.

" Maliciously perverted incident ! "

Snarled the retort, when this was told at Vire :

" The man paid mere devotion as he passed,

Knelt decently at just each wayside shrine ! "

Alas, my lawyer, I trudged yesterday—

On my two feet, and with both eyes wide ope,—

The distance, and could find no shrine at all !

According to his lights, I praise the man.

Enough ! incessant was devotion, say—

With her, you know of, praying at his side.

Still, there be relaxations of the tense :

Or life indemnifies itself for strain,

Or finds its very strain grow feebleness.

Monsieur Léonce Miranda's days were passed

Much as of old, in simple work and play.

His first endeavour, on recovery

From that sad ineffectual sacrifice,

Had been to set about repairing loss :

Never admitting, loss was to repair.

No word at any time escaped his lips

—Betrayed a lurking presence, in his heart,

Of sorrow ; no regret for mischief done—

Punishment suffered, he would rather say.

Good-tempered school-boy-fashion, he preferred

To laugh away his flogging, fair price paid

For pleasure out of bounds : if needs must be,

Get pleasure and get flogged a second time !

A sullen subject would have nursed the scars

And made excuse, for throwing grammar by,

That bench was grown uneasy to the seat.

No : this poor fellow cheerfully got hands

Fit for his stumps, and what hands failed to do,

The other members did in their degree—

Unwonted service.   With his mouth alone

He wrote, nay, painted pictures—think of that !

He played on a piano pedal-keyed,

Kicked out—if it was Bach's—good music thence.

He rode, that's readily conceivable,

But then he shot and never missed his bird,

With other feats as dexterous : I infer

He was not ignorant what hands are worth,

When he resolved on ruining his own.

So the two years passed somehow—who shall say

Foolishly,—as one estimates mankind,

The work they do, the play they leave undone ?—

Two whole years spent in that experiment

I told you of, at Clairvaux all the time,

From April on to April : why that month

More than another, notable in life ?

Does the awakening of the year arouse

Man to new projects, nerve him for fresh feats

Of what proves, for the most part of mankind

Playing or working, novel folly too ?

At any rate, I see no slightest sign

Of folly (let me tell you in advance)

Nothing but wisdom meets me manifest

In the procedure of the Twentieth Day

Of April, 'Seventy,—folly's year in France.

It was delightful Spring, and out of doors

Temptation to adventure.   Walk or ride ?

There was a wild young horse to exercise,

And teach the way to go and pace to keep :

Monsieur Léonce Miranda chose to ride.

So, while they clapped soft saddle straight on
    back,

And bitted jaw to satisfaction,—since

The partner of his days must stay at home,

Teazed by some trifling legacy of March

To throat or shoulder,—visit duly paid

And " farewell " given and received again,—

As chamber-door considerately closed

Behind him, still five minutes were to spend.

How better, than by clearing, two and two,

The staircase-steps and coming out aloft

Upon the platform yonder (raise your eyes !)

And tasting, just as those two years before,

Spring's bright advance upon the tower a-top,

The feature of the front, the Belvedere?

Look at it for a moment while I breathe.

IV

Ready to hear the rest?   How good you are !

Now for this Twentieth splendid day of Spring,

All in a tale,—sun, wind, sky, earth and sea,—

To bid man, " Up, be doing ! " Mount the stair,

Monsieur Léonce Miranda mounts so brisk,

And look—ere his elastic foot arrive—

Your longest, far and wide, o'er fronting space.

Yon white streak—Havre lighthouse ! Name and name,

How the mind runs from each to each relay,

Town after town, till Paris' self be touched,'

Superlatively big with life and death

To all the world, that very day perhaps !

But who stepped out upon the platform here,

Pinnacled over the expanse, gave thought

Neither to Rouher nor Ollivier, Roon

Nor Bismarck, Emperor nor King, but just

To steeple, church, and shrine, The Ravissante!

He saw Her, whom myself saw, but when Spring

Was passing into Fall : not robed and crowned

As, thanks to him, and her you know about,

She stands at present ; but She smiled the same.

Thither he turned—to never turn away.

He thought . .

(Suppose I should prefer " He said?"

Along with every act—and speech is act—

There go, a multitude impalpable

To ordinary human faculty,

The thoughts which give the act significance.

Who is a poet needs must apprehend

Alike both speech and thoughts which prompt to speak.

Part these, and thought withdraws to poetry :

Speech is reported in' the newspaper.)

He said, then, probably no word at all,

But thought as follows—in a minute's space—

One particle of·ore beats out such leaf !

" This Spring-morn, I am forty-three years old :

In prime of life, perfection of estate

Bodily, mental,. nay, material too,—

My very worldly fortunes reach their height.

Body and soul alike on eminence :

It is not probable I ever raise

Soul above standard by increase of worth,

Nor reasonably may expect to lift

Body beyond the present altitude.

"Behold me, Lady called The Ravissante!

Such as I am, I—gave myself to you

So long since, that I cannot say ' I give.'

All my belongings, what is summed in life,

I have submitted wholly—as man might,

At least, as *I* might, who am weak, not strong,—

Wholly, then, to your rule and governance,

So far as I had strength.   My weakness was—

I felt a fascination, at each point

And pore of me, a Power as absolute

Claiming, my soul should recognise her sway.

O you were no whit clearlier Queen, I see,

Throughout the life that rolls out ribbon-like

Its shot-silk length behind me, than the strange

Mystery—how shall I denominate

The unrobed One ? Robed you go and crowned as well,

Named by the nations : she is hard to name,

Though you have spelt out certain characters

Obscure upon what fillet binds her brow,

Lust of the flesh, lust of the eye, life's pride.

' So call her, and contemn the enchantress ! '—' Crush

The despot, and recover liberty ! '

Cry despot and enchantress at each ear.

You were conspicuous and pre-eminent,

Authoritative and imperial,—you

Spoke first, claimed homage : did I hesitate ?

Born for no mastery, but servitude,

I cannot serve two masters, says the Book ;

Master should measure strength with master, then,

Before the servant be imposed a task.

You spoke first, promised best, and threatened most ;

The other never threatened, promised, spoke

A single word, but, when your part was done,

Lifted a finger, and I, prostrate, knew

Films were about me, though you stood aloof

Smiling or frowning ' Where is power like mine

To punish or reward thee ?   Rise, thou fool !

Will to be free, and, lo, I lift thee loose !'

Did I not will, and could I rise a whit ?

Lay I, at any time, content to lie ?

' To lie, at all events, brings pleasure : make

Amends by undemanded pain !' I said.

Did not you prompt me ? 'Purchase now by pain

Pleasure hereafter in the world to come !'

I could not pluck my heart out, as you bade :

Unbidden, I burned off my hands at least.

My soul retained its treasure ; but my purse

Lightened itself with much alacrity.

Well, where is the reward ? what promised fruit

Of sacrifice in peace, content ? what sense

Of added strength to bear or to forbear ?

What influx of new light assists me´now

Even to guess you recognise a gain

In what was loss enough to mortal me ?

But she, the less authoritative voice,

Oh, how distinct enunciating, how

Plain dealing ! Gain she gave was gain indeed !

That, you deny : that, you contemptuous call

Acorns, swine's food not man's meat ! 'Spurn the draff !'

Ay, but those life-tree apples I prefer,

Am I to die of hunger till they drop ?

Husks keep flesh from starvation, anyhow.

Give those life-apples !—one, worth woods of oak,

Worth acorns by the waggon-load,—one shoot

Through heart and brain, assurance bright and brief

That you, my Lady, my own Ravissante,

Feel, through my famine, served and satisfied,

Own me, your starveling, soldier of a sort !

Your soldier ! do I read my title clear

Even to call myself your friend, not foe ?

What is the pact between us but a truce ?

At best I shall have staved off enmity,

Obtained a respite, ransomed me from wrath.

I pay, instalment by instalment, life,

Earth's tribute-money, pleasures great and small,

Whereof should at the last one penny piece

Fall short, the whole heap becomes forfeiture.

You find in me deficient soldiership :

Want the whole life or none.   I grudge that whole,

Because I am not sure of recompense :

Because I want faith.   Whose the fault ?   I ask.

If insufficient faith have done thus much,

Contributed thus much of sacrifice,

More would move mountains, you are warrant.   Well,

Grant, you, the grace, I give the gratitude !

And what were easier ?   ' Ask and have ' folk call

Miranda's method: ' Have, nor need to ask !'

So do they formulate your quality

Superlative beyond my human grace.

Q

The Ravissante, you ravish men away

From puny aches and petty pains, assuaged

By man's own art with small expenditure

Of pill or potion, unless, put to shame,

Nature is roused and sets things right herself.

Your miracles are grown our common-place ;

No day but pilgrim hobbles his last mile,

Kneels down and rises up, flings crutch away,

Or else appends it to the reverend heap

Beneath you, votive cripple-carpentry.

Some few meet failure—oh, they wanted faith,

And may betake themselves to La Salette,

Or seek Lourdes, so that hence the scandal limp !

The many get their grace and go their way

Rejoicing, with a tale to tell,—most like,

A staff to borrow, since the crutch is gone,

Should the first telling happen at my house,

And teller wet his whistle with my wine.

I tell this to a doctor and he laughs :

' Give me permission to cry—Out of bed,

You loth rheumatic sluggard ! Cheat yon chair

Of laziness, its gouty occupant !—

You should see miracles performed !   But now,

I give advice, and take as fee ten francs,

And do as much as does your Ravissante.

Send her that case of cancer to be cured,

I have refused to treat for any fee,

Bring back my would-be patient sound and whole,

And see me laugh on t' other side my mouth ! '

Can he be right, and are you hampered thus ?

Such pettiness restricts a miracle

Wrought by the Great Physician, who hears prayer,

Visibly seated in your mother-lap?

He, out of nothing, made sky, earth, and sea,

And all that in them is, man, beast, bird, fish,

Down to this insect on my parapet.

Look how the marvel of a minim crawls!

Were I to kneel among the halt and maimed,

And pray 'Who mad'st the insect with ten legs,

Make me one finger grow where ten were once!'

The very priests would thrust me out of church.

'What folly does the madman dare expect?

No faith obtains—in this late age, at least—

Such cure as that! We ease rheumatics, though!'

" Ay, bring the early ages back again,

What prodigy were unattainable?

I read your annals.   Here came Louis Onze,

Gave thrice the sum he ever gave before

At one time, some three hundred crowns, to wit—

On pilgrimage to pray for—health, he found?

Did he? I do not read it in Commines.

Here sent poor joyous Marie-Antoinette

To thank you that a Dauphin dignified,

Her motherhood—since Duke of Normandy

And Martyr of the Temple, much the same

As if no robe of hers had dressed you rich,

No silver lamps, she gave, illumed your shrine!

Here, following example, fifty years

Ago, in gratitude for birth again

Of yet another destined King of France,

Did not the Duchess fashion with her hands,

And frame in gold and crystal, and present

A bouquet made of artificial flowers?

And was he King of France, and is not he

Still Count of Chambord?

                    " Such the days of faith,

And such their produce to encourage mine !

What now, if I too count without my host?

I too have given money, ornament,

And ' artificial flowers '—which, when I plucked,

Seemed rooting at my heart and real enough:

What if I gain thereby nor health of mind,

Nor youth renewed which perished in its prime,

Burnt to a cinder 'twixt the red-hot bars,

Nor gain to see my second baby-hope

Of managing to live on terms with both

Opposing potentates, the Power and you,

Crowned with success, but dawdle out my days

In exile here at Clairvaux, with mock love,

That gives, while whispering 'Would I dared refuse !'—

What the loud voice declares my heart's free gift !

Mock worship, mock superiority

O'er those I style the world's benighted ones,

That irreligious sort I pity so,

Dumas and even Hertford, who is Duke ?

" Impiety?   Not if I know myself !

Not if you know the heart and soul, I bare,

I bid you cut, hack, slash, anatomize,

Till peccant part be found and flung away !

Demonstrate where I need more faith !   Describe

What act shall evidence sufficiency

Of faith, your warrant for such exercise

Of power, in my behalf, as all the world

Except poor praying me, declares profuse?

Poor me?   It is that world, not me alone,

That world which prates of fixed laws and the like,

I fain would save, poor world so ignorant!

And your part were—what easy miracle?

Oh, Lady, could I make your want like mine!"

Then his face grew one luminosity.

"Simple, sufficient! Happiness at height!

I solve the riddle, I persuade mankind.

I have been just the simpleton who stands—

Summoned to claim his patrimonial rights,—

At shilly-shally, may he knock or no

At his own door in his own house and home

Whereof he holds the very title-deeds!

Here is my title to this property,

This power you hold for profit of myself

And all the world at need—which need is now !

" My title—let me hear who controverts! .

Count Mailleville built yon church.   Why did he so?

Because he found your image.   How came that ?

His shepherd told him that a certain sheep

Was wont to scratch with hoof and scrape with horn

At ground where once the Danes had razed a church.

Thither he went, and there he dug, and thence

He disinterred the image he conveyed

In pomp to Londres yonder, his domain.

You liked the old place better than the new.

The Count might surely have divined as much:

He did not ; someone might have spoke a word :

No one did.   A mere dream had warned enough,

That back again in pomp you best were borne :

No dream warned, and no need of convoy was ;

An angel caught you up and clapped you down—

No mighty task, you stand one mètre high,

And people carry you about at times.

Why, then, did you despise the simple course ?

Because you are the Queen of Angels : when

You front us in a picture, there flock they,

Angels around you, here and everywhere.

" Therefore, to prove indubitable faith,

Those angels that acknowledge you their queen,

I summon them to bear me to your feet

From Clairvaux through the air, an easy trip !

Faith without flaw ! I trust your potency,

Benevolence, your will to save the world—

By such a simplest of procedures, too !

Not even by affording angel-help,

Unless it please you : there's a simpler mode :

Only suspend the law of gravity,

And, while at back, permitted to propel,

The air helps onward, let the air in front

Cease to oppose my passage through the midst!

" Thus I bestride the railing, leg o'er leg,

Thus, lo, I stand, a single inch away,

At dizzy edge of death,—no touch of fear,

As safe on tower above as turf below !

Your smile enswathes me in beatitude,

You lift along the votary—who vaults,

Who, in the twinkling of an eye, revives,

Dropt safely in the space before the church—

How crowded, since this morn is market-day !

I shall not need to speak.   The news will run

Like wild-fire.   'Thousands saw Miranda's flight !'

'Tis telegraphed to Paris in a trice.

The Boulevard is one buzz ' Do you believe ?

Well, this time, thousands saw Miranda's flight :

You know him, goldsmith in the Place Vendôme.'

In goes the Empress to the Emperor

' Now—will you hesitate to make disgorge

Your wicked King of Italy his gains,

Give the Legations to the Pope once more ? '

Which done,—why, grace goes back to operate,

They themselves set a good example first,

Resign the empire twenty years usurped,

And Henry, the Desired One, reigns o'er France !

Regenerated France makes all things new !

My house no longer stands on Quai Rousseau

But Quai rechristened Alacoque : a quai

Where Renan burns his book, and Veuillot burns

Renan beside, since Veuillot rules the roast,

Re-edits now indeed 'The Universe.'

O blessing, O superlatively big

With blessedness beyond all blessing dreamed

By man ! for just that promise has effect,

'Old things shall pass away and all be new !'

Then, for a culminating mercy-feat,

Wherefore should I dare dream impossible

That I too have my portion in the change ?

My past with all its sorrow, sin and shame,

Becomes a blank, a nothing ! There she stands,

Clara de Millefleurs, all deodorized,

Twenty years' stain wiped off her innocence !

There never was Muhlhausen, nor at all

Duke Hertford: nought that was, remains, except

The beauty,—yes, the beauty is unchanged !

Well, and the soul too, that must keep the same !

And so the trembling little virgin hand

Melts into mine, that's back again, of course !

—Think not I care about my poor old self !

I only want my hand for that one use,

To take her hand, and say 'I marry you—

Men, women, angels, you behold my wife !

There is no secret, nothing wicked here,

Nothing she does not wish the world to know !'

None of your married women have the right

To mutter 'Yes, indeed, she beats us all

In beauty,—but our lives are pure at least !'

Bear witness, for our marriage is no thing

Done in a corner ! 'Tis The Ravissante

Repairs the wrong of Paris. See, She smiles,

She beckons, She bids ' Hither, both of you ! '

And may we kneel? And will you bless us both?

And may I worship you, and yet love her?

Then ! "—

   A sublime spring from the balustrade

About the tower so often talked about,

A flash in middle air, and stone-dead lay

Monsieur Léonce Miranda on the turf.

A gardener who watched, at work the while

Dibbling a flower-bed for geranium-shoots,

Saw the catastrophe, and, straitening back,

Stood up and shook his brows. " Poor soul, poor soul

Just what I prophesied the end would be !

Ugh—the Red Night-cap ! " (as he raised the head)

" This must be what he meant by those strange words

While I was weeding larkspurs, yesterday,

' Angels would take him ! ' Mad ! "

No ! sane, I say.

Such being the conditions of his life,

Such end of life was not irrational.

Hold a belief, you only half-believe,

With all-momentous issues either way,—

And I advise you imitate this leap,

Put faith to proof, be cured or killed at once !

Call you man, killed through cutting cancer out,

The worse for such an act of bravery ?

That's more than *I* know.   In my estimate,

Better lie prostrate on his turf at peace,

Than, wistful, eye, from out the tent, the tower,

Racked with a doubt " Will going on bare knees

All the way to The Ravissante and back,

Saying my Ave Mary all the time,

Somewhat excuse if I postpone my march ?

—Make due amends for that one kiss I gave

In gratitude to her who held me out

Superior Fricquot's sermon, hot from press,

A-spread with hands so sinful yet so smooth ? ''

And now, sincerely do I pray she stand,

Clara, with interposing sweep of robe,

Between us and this horror !   Any screen

Turns white by contrast with the tragic pall ;

And her dubiety distracts at least,

R

As well as snow, from such decided black.

With womanhood, at least, we have to do :

Ending with Clara—is the word too kind ?

Let pass the shock !   There's poignancy enough

When what one parted with, a minute since,

Alive and happy, is returned a wreck—

All that was, all that seemed about to be,

Razed out and ruined now for evermore,

Because a straw descended on this scale

Rather than that, made death o'er-balance life.

But think of cage-mates in captivity,

Inured to day-long, night-long vigilance

Each of the other's tread and angry turn

When, bolt on prison-bars, a captive came

These two, society shut out, and thus

Penned in, to settle down and regulate

By the strange law, the solitary life—

When death divorces such a fellowship,

This may pair off with that prodigious woe

Imagined of a ghastly brotherhood—

One watcher left in lighthouse out at sea,

With leagues of surf between the land and him,

Alive with his dead partner on the rock ;

One galley-slave, whom curse and blow compel

To labour on at oar—beside his chain,

Encumbered with his corpse-companion now.

Such these : although, no prisoners, self-entrenched,

They kept the world off from their barricade.

Memory, gratitude was poignant, sure,

Though pride brought consolation of a kind.

Twenty years long, had Clara been—of whom

The rival, nay, the victor, past dispute?

What if in turn The Ravissante at length

Proved victor—which was doubtful—any how,

Here lay the inconstant with, conspicuous too,

The fruit of his good fortune!

              " Has he gained

By leaving me?" she might soliloquize :

" All love could do, I did for him.   I learned

By heart his nature, what he loved and loathed,

Leaned to with liking, turned from with distaste.

No matter what his least velleity,

I was determined he should want no wish,

And in conformity administered

To his requirement; most of joy I mixed

With least of sorrow in life's daily draught,

Twenty years long, life's proper average.

And when he got to quarrel with my cup,

Would needs out-sweeten honey, and discard

That gall-drop we require lest nectar cloy,—

I did not call him fool, and vex my friend,

But quietly allowed experiment,

Encouraged him to dust his drink, and now

Grate *lignum vitæ*, now bruise so-called grains

Of Paradise, and now, for perfume, pour

Distilment rare, the rose of Jericho,

Holy-thorn, passion-flower, and what know I?

Till beverage obtained the fancied smack.

'Twas wild-flower-wine that neither helped nor harmed.

Who sipped and held it for restorative—

What harm? But here has he been through the hedge

Straying in search of simples, while my back

Was turned a minute, and he finds a prize,

Monkshood and belladonna! O my child,

My truant little boy, despite the beard,

The body two feet broad and six feet long,

And what the calendar counts middle age—

You wanted, did you, to enjoy a flight?

Why not have taken into confidence

Me, that was mother to you?—never mind

What mock disguise of mistress held you mine!

Had you come laughing, crying, with request,

' Make me fly, mother!' I had run upstairs

And held you tight the while I danced you high

In air from tower-top, singing ' Off we go

(On pilgrimage to Lourdes some day next month)

And swift we soar (to Rome with Peter-pence)

And low we light (at Paris where we pick

Another jewel from our store of stones

And send it for a present to the Pope) !'

So, dropt indeed you were, but on my knees,

Rolling and crowing, not a bit the worse

For journey to your Ravissante and back.

Now, no more Clairvaux—which I made you

    build,

And think an inspiration of your own—

No more fine house, trim garden, pretty park,

Nothing I used to busy you about,

And make believe you worked for my surprise

What weariness to me will work become

Now that I need not seem surprised again !

This boudoir, for example, with the doves

(My stupid maid has damaged, dusting one)

Embossed in stucco o'er the looking-glass

Beside the toilet-table ! dear—dear me ! "

Here she looked up from her absorbing grief,

And round her, crow-like grouped, the Cousinry,

(She grew aware) sat witnesses at watch.

For, two days had elapsed since fate befell

The courser in the meadow, stretched so stark.

They did not cluster on the tree-tops, close

Their sooty ranks, caw and confabulate

For nothing : but, like calm determined crows,

They came to take possession of their corpse.

And who shall blame them ?   Had not they the right ?

One spoke.   " They would be gentle, not austere.

They understood, and were compassionate.

Madame Muhlhausen lay too abject now

For aught but the sincerest pity ; still,

Since plain speech salves the wound it seems to make,

They must speak plainly—circumstances spoke !

Sin had conceived and brought forth death indeed.

As the commencement, so the close of things :

Just what might be expected all along !

Monsieur Léonce Miranda launched his youth

Into a cesspool of debauchery,

And, if he thence emerged all dripping slime,

—" Where was the change except from thin to thick,

One warm rich mud-bath, Madame ?—you, in place

Of Paris-drainage and distilment, you,

He never needed budge from, boiled to rags !

True, some good instinct left the natural man,

Some touch of that deep dye wherewith imbued

By education, in his happier day,

The hopeful offspring of high parentage

Was fleece-marked moral and religious sheep,—

Some ruddle, faint remainder, (we admit)

Stuck to Miranda, rubbed he ne'er so rude

Against the goatly coarseness : to the last,

Moral he styled himself, religious too !

Which means—what ineradicable good,

You found, you never left till good's self proved

Perversion and distortion, nursed to growth

So monstrous, that the tree-stock, dead and dry,

Were seemlier far than such a heap grotesque

Of fungous flourishing excrescence.   Here,

Sap-like affection, meant for family,

Stole off to feed one sucker fat—yourself ;

While branchage, trained religiously aloft

To rear its head in reverence to the sun,

Was pulled down earthward, pegged and picketed,

By topiary contrivance, till the tree

Became an arbour where, at vulgar ease,

Sat superstition grinning through the loops.

Still, nature is too strong or else too weak

For cockney treatment : either, tree springs back

To pristine shape, or else degraded droops,

And turns to touchwood at the heart. So here—

Body and mind, at last the man gave way.

His body—there it lies, what part was left

Unmutilated ! for, the strife commenced

Two years ago, when, both hands burnt to ash,

A branch broke loose, by loss of what choice twigs!

As for his mind—behold our register

Of all its moods, from the incipient mad,

Nay, mere erratic, to the stark insane,

Absolute idiocy or what is worse !

All have we catalogued—extravagance

In worldly matters, luxury absurd,

And zeal as crazed in its expenditure

Of nonsense called devotion.   Don't we know

—We Cousins, bound in duty to our kin,—

What mummeries were practised by you two

At Clairvaux ?   Not a servant got discharge

But came and told his grievance, testified

To acts which turn religion to a farce.

And as the private mock, so patent—see—

The public scandal ! Ask the neighbourhood—

Or rather, since we asked them long ago,

Read what they answer, depositions down,

Signed, sealed and sworn to ! Brief, the man was mad.

We are his heirs and claim our heritage

Madame Muhlhausen,—whom good taste forbids

We qualify as do these documents,—

Fear not lest justice stifle mercy's prayer !

True, had you lent a willing ear at first,

Had you obeyed our call two years ago,

Restrained a certain insolence of eye,

A volubility of tongue, that time,

Your prospects had been none the worse, perhaps.

Still, fear not but a decent competence

Shall smooth the way for your declining age !

What we propose, then . ."

                            Clara dried her eyes,

Sat up, surveyed the consistory, spoke,

After due pause, with something of a smile.

" Gentlemen, kinsfolk of my friend defunct,

In thus addressing me—of all the world !—

You much misapprehend what part I play.

I claim no property you speak about.

You might as well address the park-keeper,

Harangue him on some plan advisable

For covering the park with cottage-plots.

He is the servant, no proprietor,

His business is to see the sward kept trim,

Untrespassed over by the indiscreet :

Beyond that, he refers you to myself—

Another servant of another kind—

Who again—quite as limited in act—

Refer you, with your projects,—can I else ?

To who in mastery is ultimate,

The Church.   The Church is sole administrant,

Since sole possessor of what worldly wealth

Monsieur Léonce Miranda late possessed.,

Often enough has he attempted, nay,

Forced me, well-nigh, to occupy the post

You seemingly suppose I fill,—receive

As gift the wealth entrusted me as grace.

This—for quite other reasons than appear

So cogent to your perspicacity,—

This I refused ; and, firm as you could wish,

Still was my answer 'We two understand

Each one the other.   I am intimate

—As how can be mere fools and knaves—or, say,

Even your Cousins ?—with your love to me,

Devotion to the Church.   Would Providence

Appoint, and make me certain of the same,

That I survive you (which is little like,

Seeing you hardly overpass my age

And more than match me in abundant health)

In such case, certainly I would accept ·

Your bounty: better I than alien hearts

Should execute your planned benevolence

To man, your proposed largess to the Church.

But though I be survivor,—weakly frame,

With only woman's wit to make amends,—

When I shall die, or while I am alive,

Cannot you figure me an easy mark

For hypocritical rapacity,

Kith, kin and generation, couching low,

Ever on the alert to pounce on prey?

Far be it I should say they profited

By that first frenzy-fit themselves induced,—

Cold-blooded scenical buffoons at sport

With horror and damnation o'er a grave:

That were too shocking—I absolve them there!

Nor did they seize the moment of your swoon

To rifle pocket, wring a paper thence,

Their Cousinly dictation, and enrich

Thereby each mother's son as heart could wish,

Had nobody supplied a codicil.

But when the pain, poor friend! had prostrated

Your body, though your soul was right again,

I fear they turned your weakness to account!

Why else to me, who agonizing watched,

Sneak, cap in hand, now bribe me to forsake

My maimed Léonce, now bully, cap on head,

The impudent pretension to assuage

Such sorrows as demanded Cousin's care?—

For you rejected, hated, fled me, far

In foreign lands you laughed at me!—they judged.

And, think you, will the unkind ones hesitate

S

To try conclusions with my helplessness,—

To pounce on, misuse me, your derelict,

Helped by advantage that bereavement lends

Folks, who, while yet you lived, played tricks like these?

You only have to die, and they detect,

In all you said and did, insanity!

Your faith was fetish-worship, your regard

For Christ's prime precept which endows the poor

And strips the rich, a craze from first to last!

They so would limn your likeness, paint your life,

That if it ended by some accident,—

For instance, if, attempting to arrange

The plants below that dangerous Belvedere

I cannot warn you from sufficiently,

You lost your balance and fell headlong—fine

Occasion, such, for crying *Suicide!*

Non compos mentis, naturally next,

Hands over Clairvaux to a Cousin-tribe

Who nor like me nor love The Ravissante,

Therefore be ruled by both ! Life-interest

In Clairvaux,—conservation, guardianship

Of earthly good for heavenly purpose,—give

Such and no other proof of confidence !

Let Clara represent the Ravissante ! '

—To whom accordingly, he then and there

Bequeathed each stick and stone, by testament

In holograph, mouth managing the quill :

Go, see the same in Londres, if you doubt !"

Then smile grew laugh, as sudden up she stood

And out she spoke : intemperate the speech !

"And now, sirs, for your special courtesy,

Your candle held up to the character

Of Lucie Steiner, whom you qualify

As coming short of perfect womanhood.

Yes, kindly critics, truth for once you tell !

True is it that through childhood, poverty,

Sloth, pressure of temptation, I succumbed,

And, ere I found what honor meant, lost mine.

So was the sheep lost, which the Shepherd found

And never lost again.   My friend found me;

Or better say, the Shepherd found us both—

Since he, my friend, was much in the same mire

When first we made acquaintance.   Each helped each,—

A two-fold extrication from the slough ;

And, saving me, he saved himself.   Since then,

Unsmirched we kept our cleanliness of coat.

It is his perfect constancy, you call!

My friend's main fault—he never left his love!

While as for me, I dare your worst, impute

One breach of loving bond, these twenty years,

To me whom only cobwebs bound, you count !

'He was religiously disposed in youth !'

That may be, though we did not meet at church.

Did he become Voltairian like your scamps,

Under my teaching, fools who mock his faith?

'Infirm of body !' I am silent there :

Even yourselves acknowledge service done,

Whatever motive your own souls supply

As inspiration.   Love made labour light."

Then laugh grew frown, and frown grew terrible.

Do recollect what sort of person shrieked—

" Such was I, saint or sinner, what you please:

And who is it casts stone at me but you?

By your own showing, sirs, you bought and

    sold,

Took what advantage bargain promised bag,

Abundantly did business, and with whom ?

Miranda !—you pronounce imbecile, push

Indignantly aside if he presume

To settle his affairs like other folk !

How is it you have stepped into his shoes,

And stand there, bold as brass, ' Miranda, late

Now, Firm-Miranda ?'   Sane, he signed away

That little birthright, did he ?   Hence to trade !

I know you, and he knew who dipped and ducked,

Truckled and played the parasite in vain,

As now one, now the other, here you cringed,

Were feasted, took our presents, you—those drops,

Just for your wife's adornment ! you—that spray

Exactly suiting, as most diamonds do,

Your daughter on her marriage ! No word then

Of somebody the wanton ! Hence, I say,

Subscribers to the 'Siècle,' every snob—

For here the post brings me the 'Univers'!

Home and make money in the Place Vendôme,

Sully yourselves no longer by my sight,

And, when next Schneider wants a new *parure*,

Be careful lest you stick there by mischance

That stone beyond compare entrusted you

To kindle faith with, when, Miranda's gift,

Crowning the very crown, the Ravissante

Shall claim it ! As to Clairvaux—talk to Her !

She answers by the Chapter of Raimbaux ! "

Vituperative, truly ! All this wrath

Because the man's relations thought him mad !

Whereat, I hope you see the Cousinry

Turn each to other, blankly dolorous,

Consult a moment, more by shrug and shrug

Than mere man's language,—finally conclude

To leave the reprobate untroubled now

In her unholy triumph, till the Law

Shall right the injured ones; for gentlemen

Allow the female sex, this sort at least,

Its privilege.   So, simply " Cockatrice!"—

" Jezebel !"—" Queen of the Camellias !"—cried

Cousin to cousin, as yon hinge a-creak

Shut out the party, and the gate returned

To custody of Clairvaux.   " Pretty place !

What say you, when it proves our property,

To trying a concurrence with La Roche,

And laying down a rival oyster-bed ?

Where the park ends, the sea begins, you know."

So took they comfort till they came to Vire.

But I would linger, fain to snatch a look

At Clara as she stands in pride of place,

Somewhat more satisfying than my glance

So furtive, so near futile, yesterday,

Because one must be courteous. Ot the masks

That figure in this little history,

She only has a claim to my respect,

And one-eyed, in her French phrase, rules the blind.

Miranda hardly did his best with life :

He might have opened eye, exerted brain,

Attained conception as to right and law

In certain points respecting intercourse

Of man with woman—love, one likes to say;

Which knowledge had dealt rudely with the claim

Of Clara to play representative

And from perdition rescue soul, forsooth!

Also, the sense of him should have sufficed

For building up some better theory

Of how God operates in heaven and earth,

Than would establish Him participant

In doings yonder at the Ravissante.

The heart was wise according to its lights

And limits; but the head refused more sun,

And shrank into its mew and craved less space.

Clara, I hold the happier specimen,—

It may be, through that artist-preference

For work complete, inferiorly proposed,

To incompletion, though it aim aright.

  Morally, no! Aspire, break bounds! I say,

Endeavour to be good, and better still,

And best ! Success is nought, endeavour's all.

But intellect adjusts the means to ends,

Tries the low thing, and leaves it done, at least ;

No prejudice to high thing, intellect

Would do and will do, only give the means.

Miranda, in my picture-gallery,

Presents a Blake ; be Clara—Meissonnier !

Merely considered so, by artist, mind !

For, break through Art and rise to poetry,

Bring Art to tremble nearer, touch enough

The verge of vastness to inform our soul

What orb makes transit through the dark above,

And there's the triumph!—there the incomplete,

More than completion, matches the immense,—

Then, Michelagnolo against the world !

With this proviso, let me study her

Approvingly, the finished little piece !

Born, bred, with just one instinct,—that of growth:

Her quality was, caterpillar-like,

To all-unerringly select a leaf

And without intermission feed her fill,

Become the Painted Peacock, or belike

The Brimstone-wing, when time of year should suit ;

And 'tis a sign (say entomologists)

Of sickness, when the creature stops its meal

One minute, either to look up at heaven,

Or turn aside for change of aliment.

No doubt there was a certain ugliness

In the beginning, as the grub grew worm :

She could not find the proper plant at once,

But crawled and tumbled through a whole parterre.

Husband Muhlhausen served for stuff not long :

Then came confusion of the slimy track

From London, " where she gave the tone awhile,"

To Paris : let the stalks start up again,

Now she is off them, all the greener they !

But, settled on Miranda, how she sucked,

Assimilated juices, took the tint,

Mimicked the form and texture of her food !

Was he for pastime ?   Who so frolic-fond

As Clara ?   Had he a devotion-fit ?

Clara grew serious with like qualm, be sure !

In health and strength he,—healthy too and strong,

She danced, rode, drove, took pistol-practice, fished,

Nay, " managed sea-skiff with consummate skill."

In pain and weakness, he,—she patient watched

And wiled the slow drip-dropping hours away

She bound again the broken self-respect,

She picked out the true meaning from mistake,

Praised effort in each stumble, laughed "Well-climbed!"

When others groaned "None ever grovelled so!"

" Rise, you have gained experience!" was her word :

" Lie satisfied, the ground is just your place ! "

They thought appropriate counsel.   " Live, not die,

And take my full life to eke out your own :

That shall repay me and with interest !

Write !—is your mouth not clever as my hand ?

Paint !—the last Exposition warrants me,

Plenty of people must ply brush with toes.

And as for music—look, what folks nickname

A lyre, those ancients played to ravishment,—

Over the pendule, see, Apollo grasps

A three-stringed gimcrack which no Liszt could
   coax

Such music from as jews-harp makes to-day!

Do your endeavour like a man, and leave

The rest to 'fortune who assists the bold'—

Learn, you, the Latin which you taught me first,

You clever creature—clever, yes, I say ! "

If he smiled " Let us love, love's wrong comes right,

Shows reason last of all ! Necessity

Must meanwhile serve for plea—so, mind not much

Old Fricquot's menace ! "—back she smiled " Who

    minds ? "

If he sighed " Ah, but She is strict, they say,

For all Her mercy at the Ravissante,

She scarce will be put off so ! "—straight a sigh

Returned " My lace must go to trim Her gown ! "

I nowise doubt she inwardly believed

Smiling and sighing had the same effect

Upon the venerated image.   What,

She did believe in, I as little doubt,

Was—Clara, and her birthright to sustain

Existence, grow from grub to butterfly,

Upon unlimited Miranda-leaf;

In which prime article of faith confirmed,

According to capacity, she fed

On and on till the leaf was eaten up,

That April morning.   Even then, I praise

Her forethought which prevented leafless stalk

Bestowing any hoarded succulence

On earwig and blackbeetle squat beneath ;—

Clairvaux, that stalk whereto her hermitage

She tacked by golden throw of silk, so fine,

So anything but feeble, that her sleep

Inside it, through last winter, two years long,

Recked little of the storm and strife without.

" But—loved him?" Friend, I do not praise her love !

True love works never for the loved one so,

Nor spares skin-surface, smoothening truth away.

Love bids touch truth, endure truth, and embrace

Truth, though, embracing truth, love crush itself.

" Worship not me, but God!" the angels urge :

That is love's grandeur : still, in pettier love

The nice eye can distinguish grade and grade.

Shall mine degrade the velvet green and puce

Of caterpillar, palmer-worm—or what—

Ball in and out of ball, each ball with brush

Of Venus' eye-fringe round the turquoise egg

That nestles soft,—compare such paragon

With any scarabæus of the brood

That, born to fly, keeps wing in wing-case, walks

Persistently a-trundling dung on earth ?

T

Egypt may venerate such hierophants,

Not I—the couple yonder, Father Priest

And Mother Nun, who came and went and came,

Beset this Clairvaux, trundled money-muck

To midden and the main heap oft enough,

But never bade unshut from sheath the gauze,

Nor showed that, who would fly, should let fall filth,

Warning " Your jewel, brother, is a blotch:

Sister, your lace trails ordure.   Leave your sins,

And so best gift the Crown and grace the Robe ! "

The superstition is extinct, you hope ?

It were, with my good will !   Suppose it so,

Bethink you likewise of the latest use

Whereto a Night-cap is convertible,

And draw your very thickest, thread and thrum,

O'er such a decomposing face of things,

Once so alive, it seemed immortal too!

This happened two years since.   The Cousinry

Returned to Paris, called in help from Law,   .

And in due form proceeded to dispute

Monsieur Léonce Miranda's competence,

Being insane, to make a valid Will.

Much testimony volunteered itself;

The issue hardly could be doubtful—but

For that sad 'Seventy which must intervene,

Provide poor France with other work to mind

Than settling lawsuits, even for the sake

Of such a party as the Ravissante.

It only was this Summer that the case

Could come and be disposed of, two weeks since,

At Vire—Tribunal Civil—Chamber First.

Here, issued with all regularity,

I hold the judgment—just, inevitable,

Nowise to be contested by what few

Can judge the judges ; sum and substance, thus—

" Inasmuch as we find, the Cousinry,

During that very period when they take

Monsieur Léonce Miranda for stark mad,

Considered him to be quite sane enough

For doing much important business with—

Nor showed suspicion of his competence

Until, by turning of the tables, loss

Instead of gain accrued to them thereby,—

Plea of incompetence we set aside.

—" The rather, that the dispositions, sought

To be impugned, are natural and right,

Nor jar with any reasonable claim

Of kindred, friendship or acquaintance here.

Nobody is despoiled, none overlooked;

Since the testator leaves his property

To just that person whom, of all the world,

He counted he was most indebted to.

In mere discharge, then, of conspicuous debt,

Madame Muhlhausen has priority,

Enjoys the usufruct of Clairvaux.

        " Next,

Such debt discharged, such life determining,

Such earthly interest provided for,

Monsieur Léonce Miranda may bequeath,

In absence of more fit recipient, fund

And usufruct together to the Church

Whereof he was a special devotee.

" —Which disposition, being consonant

With a long series of such acts' and deeds

Notorious in his life-time, needs must stand,

Unprejudiced by eccentricity

Nowise amounting to distemper : since,

In every instance signalized as such,

We recognise no over-leaping bounds,

No straying out of the permissible :

Duty to the Religion of the Land,—

Neither excessive nor inordinate.

" The minor accusations are dismissed ;

They prove mere freak and fancy, boyish mood

In age mature of simple kindly man.

Exuberant in generosities

To all the world : no fact confirms the fear

He meditated mischief to himself

That morning when he met the accident

Which ended fatally.   The case is closed."

How otherwise?   So, when I grazed the skirts,

And had the glimpse of who made, yesterday,—

Woman and retinue of goats and sheep,—

The sombre path one whiteness, vision-like,

As out of gate, and in at gate again,

They wavered,—she was lady there for life :

And, after life—I hope, a white success

Of some sort, wheresoever life resume

School interrupted by vacation—death ;

Seeing that home she goes with prize in hand,

Confirmed the Châtelaine of Clairvaux.

True,

Such prize fades soon to insignificance.

Though she have eaten her Miranda up,

And spun a cradle-cone through which she pricks

Her passage, and proves peacock-butterfly,

This Autumn—wait a little week of cold !

Peacock and death's-head-moth end much the same.

And could she still continue spinning,—sure,

Cradle would soon crave shroud for substitute,

And o'er this life of her's distaste would drop

Red-cotton-Night-cap-wise.

How say you, friend?

Have I redeemed my promise? Smile assent

Through the dark Winter-gloom between us both!

Already, months ago and miles away,

I just as good as told you, in a flash,

The while we paced the sands before my house,

All this poor story—truth and nothing else.

Accept that moment's flashing, amplified,

Impalpability reduced to speech,

Conception proved by birth,—no other change!

Can what Saint-Rambert flashed me in a thought,

Good gloomy London make a poem of?

Such ought to be whatever dares precede,

Play ruddy herald-star to your white blaze

About to bring us day. How fail imbibe

Some foretaste of effulgence? Sun shall wax,

And star shall wane : what matter, so star tell

The drowsy world to start awake, rub eyes,

And stand all ready for morn's joy a-blush?

January 23, 1873.

LONDON: PRINTED BY
SPOTTISWOODE AND CO., NEW-STREET SQUARE
AND PARLIAMENT STREET